COUNTDOWN TO DANGER

CHOOSE YOUR OWN ENDING!

For Danielle, Ruby and Léo . . .
always my first choice in the adventure of life!

Scholastic Canada Ltd.
604 King Street West, Toronto, Ontario M5V 1E1, Canada

Scholastic Inc.
557 Broadway, New York, NY 10012, USA

Scholastic Australia Pty Limited
PO Box 579, Gosford, NSW 2250, Australia

Scholastic New Zealand Limited
Private Bag 94407, Botany, Manukau 2163, New Zealand

Scholastic Children's Books
Euston House, 24 Eversholt Street, London NW1 1DB, UK

www.scholastic.ca

Library and Archives Canada Cataloguing in Publication

Title: Canadian sabotage / Jeff Szpirglas.
Names: Szpirglas, Jeff, author.
Description: Series statement: Countdown to danger: choose your ending!
Identifiers: Canadiana (print) 2019020401X | Canadiana (ebook) 20190204036 | ISBN 9781443182379
(softcover) | ISBN 9781443182386 (ebook)
Subjects: LCSH: Plot-your-own stories. | LCGFT: Choose-your-own stories.
Classification: LCC PS8637.Z65 C36 2020 | DDC jC813/.6—dc23

Photos ©: cover: Shutterstock.com; cover timer: milmirko/Getty Images; cover border: Rochakred/Dreamstime;
i bottom and throughout: Evgeniy yes/Shutterstock; 1 clock and throughout: Samarskaya/Getty Images;
140 border: Rochakred/Dreamstime.

6 5 4 3 2 1   Printed in Canada 114   20 21 22 23 24

JEFF SZPIRGLAS

COUNTDOWN TO DANGER

CHOOSE YOUR OWN ENDING!

CANADIAN SABOTAGE

Scholastic Canada Ltd.
Toronto New York London Auckland Sydney
Mexico City New Delhi Hong Kong Buenos Aires

30:00

Your eyes snap open and you look around. This can't be. You're bobbing in the rough, frigid waters of the Atlantic Ocean. Alone.

You spin around, trying to get your bearings. How did you get here?

Your mind is cloudy. You dig deeper, and flashes of memory punch through your mental haze. Something happened with your parents. Your dad, a cartographer with the university, took you on this trip to the Maritimes. He'd brought that weird old map with him. Took you and your mom on a fishing tour. Captain somebody, you vaguely remember. Then he told you the boat driver wasn't safe.

Everything goes foggy again. And not just your thoughts. A bank of fog is rolling in. You stare through the billowing whiteness and notice something else. There's a rocky outcrop with a lighthouse on it. Maybe you could swim to that.

And now you see two boats not too far away. You're pretty sure one of them is an anchored dive boat. The other is a speedboat cutting through the water towards you.

You search your pockets for your cellphone,

although it's soaked and useless. That's when you feel something beneath your shirt. You pull out a parcel wrapped in plastic, then realize what you're holding.

"The map," you whisper.

It's what your parents had been so worried about.

Follow the map, you recall your dad telling you. He'd been insistent. *Find the treasure! That will be the key to finding us.*

But where did your parents go? You search the ocean around you. "Mom? Dad?!" you call out. Nothing.

You close your eyes, straining to filter through your memories. There's a flash of the boat driver. Another flash—your mom slipping you the map, telling you to trust no one and not to worry about her and your dad. *"Just get to the treasure first, kiddo."*

Something clunking you on the head.

You're pretty sure your parents are safe, because whoever was after them wanted this map—and the treasure. And your mom and dad seemed to know what they were doing. At least you hope so.

For the moment you tread water, weighing your options.

If you head to the lighthouse, turn to page 24.

If you'd rather wait for the speedboat, turn to page 69.

If you try the boat just up ahead, turn to page 106.

Erin is consumed with the treasure chest—so consumed that you can probably get to her boat with the pilot. Whoever's got control of the boat will have control of the situation, which is quickly burning out of control.

You quickly agree to the pilot's proposition and continue to lead the way to the boat. You catch a glimpse of Erin fiddling with the chest, and then the waves take you back down and she disappears from view.

Bob.

Now she's hammering the lock with a heavy rock.

Bob.

Then she's throwing the lock away.

Bob.

But you're at the boat now!

Holding out your free hand, you wait for the waves to push you up the side of the boat. You grab it with one hand and try to hold on as best you can. The wave pulls back, and you're in a tug-of-war between the boat and the pilot. As you're trying to decide which to let go of, a wave pushes the pilot up. In one smooth move, you pull with all your might. He manages to grab hold of the ledge, and you both spill onto the deck.

"Erin!" you shout.

But Erin isn't looking at or listening to you. She's heaving on the lid of the chest.

Erin yanks the lid off the chest, and—

A luminous green glow pours out of it.

"What the—?"

Suddenly, the light is so bright, so intense, that you're forced to turn away. You drop to the deck of the boat, where the pilot is resting. You cover your eyes, blinking hard. Even then, it's impossible to fully escape the burning, blinding light.

And then, as soon as it began, the light fades.

When you feel confident enough, you blink your eyes open. The pilot is sitting beside you, looking confused.

The pair of you slowly stand up. You look over to the rocks. The chest is open. No green light can be seen. And no Erin.

You turn to the pilot. "You know . . . maybe we should try a *different* treasure," you say. "Erin can have this one."

00:00

You survived! There are eleven other ways to escape the danger— try to find them all!

You can deal with the pilot later. Right now you need to get to Erin before she gets away with everything.

"I need to go," you say, "or else Erin's going to get the treasure before us."

"Who's Erin?" the pilot asks.

"Good question," you snap back. "But I don't think she's going to wait for me to explain!"

Leaving the pilot hanging off the side of the boat, you paddle over to the sea caves.

The water pounds against the rocks, and a rogue wave grabs you, nearly slamming you face first into the hard, cold surface. You hold out your hands and brace for impact. Your face isn't smashed in, but the wind is knocked out of your lungs as you're deposited on a slick ledge. The wave pulls back, and you scramble to find your footing and shimmy over to the sea cave where Erin is busy trying to get into the treasure chest. She's using a rock to hammer away at the rusted lock.

Erin is so consumed with the treasure that she doesn't notice your presence until you're standing right over her, dripping. "Oh, it's *you*," she says. "I thought you were rescuing that pilot."

"He's okay," you say, not pointing out that the two of you almost died. Did Erin even notice *that*? Probably not, from the single-minded look on her face as she continues to smash at the lock.

Suddenly, there's a dull *thunk* as the lock falls to the ground. Erin's eyes light up maniacally. "I've done it!" she hisses. "The treasure is mi—" She stops for a moment, giving you the briefest of glances. ". . . is ours, of course."

You lean over Erin as she grasps the lid, pulls it back, and—

CLUNK!

The lid crashes on the rocks, nearly smashing your feet in the process.

You look into the dark recesses of the chest but see nothing. You lean in for a closer look. You still can't see anything. Erin sticks her head right in.

"What's there?" you ask.

"There's . . ." she starts.

"Yes?"

"Nothing," she grumbles, shaking her head as she pulls it back out. "There's nothing there. No gold, no jewels!" She turns to you angrily. "What kind of map was this supposed to be? A treasure map or a waste of time map?"

But as you look past Erin, the chest doesn't seem to be so empty anymore. There's a green light glowing from inside it. It grabs both of your attention as you peer into the chest once again.

This time, there's a huge hunk of rock, but like no rock you've ever seen. It glows and pulses with an inner light that shifts in brightness and colour. First it's green, then yellow, then blue, then—

You can't look away.

The rock is calling to you.

You want it all to yourself. There's no need to return to your home, to find your parents. You can stay here with the rock. You reach out to touch it. Yes! Touch it! Hold it. Never take your hands off it . . .

You realize two things. One, Erin's also touching the rock, and two, neither of you can let go. So bright. So beautiful.

And yours and Erin's forever.

Whether you like it or not.

THE END.

To try again, go back to page 22.

To try again, go back to page 22.

Making sure the map is safely tucked away where Erin won't see it, you recount the basics of what you can remember: parents missing, you waking up in the ocean.

Erin nods, taking it in. "And you don't remember getting on the boat?" she says.

You shake your head. "Everything's . . . fuzzy."

"I could take you back to the mainland," Erin says. She fires up the engine and spins the boat around.

You're about to take her up on the offer, but then you signal for her to stop.

"What's up? Something you forgot to tell me?"

"No," you start, thinking aloud. "But we'll just lose time going there and having to come back out again. What if we drive along the coastline and I remember something?"

"Like what?"

You close your eyes, trying to focus, to remember. You can't quite get the images in your head, but you think you recall seeing coastline. Rocky coastline. And beyond that—old fishing huts?

"Are there any fishing villages nearby?" you ask.

Erin narrows her eyes. "There's one," she says. "But

it's abandoned. Some of the local kayak companies use it as a stopping point on their tours. But that's it."

"Take me there," you tell her.

"Sure thing." Erin speeds off along the coast.

A few minutes later, you watch as she edges the boat closer to land. Nobody lives out here. It's just open sea on one side, a craggy hill on the other. But then the boat slows down and weathered huts emerge. *This must be it*, you think.

Erin steers to an outcrop of rocks, then cuts the engine. "I can't dock here. You'll have to make your way onto land by foot," she says, pointing to the water below. "Plus, like I said: this place is abandoned. I have to get a few things done back at the mainland, but I can come get you in a couple of hours. That work for you?"

"Sure. If I'm not here, can you contact the police?"

Erin nods.

You're still not sure whether you can trust her, but at least you'll be on land, which is better than where you started this adventure. And you're following the only clue you've got.

Turn to page 104.

Thrust aboard the men's boat, you take to the sea again.

A lightning storm is rolling in, and the strong wind means you're bouncing over large, roiling waves. The boat is tossed to and fro, and it's a good thing you haven't eaten in ages, because you're pretty sure you'd be losing your lunch otherwise.

One of the men steers the boat, while the other two gear up with shovels and pickaxes as the island looms into view.

Once you reach the shoreline, they drop the anchor. You're shoved off the boat and into the water, then forced ashore to start looking for the treasure.

The man who stole your map studies it carefully. He looks around the island and points to some of the rocky outcrops by the sea. Two of them are shaped like fangs. He holds the map up to the fangs and looks back and forth between them.

"We're here," he says.

There's no trail to follow, but he seems to know where he's going. The four of you push up a hill and follow the rugged terrain.

The sky is still angry, and the landscape has an

almost skeletal feel, like you're traversing the bones of a fallen dragon.

You reach a long stone footpath that veers around a terrifying-looking swamp. Dozens of snakes scatter as you approach.

If you learned about the island from Feared Beard, turn to page 83.
If you ran away when Feared Beard tried to talk to you, turn to page 86.

You're so close. You just need to give the lid one hard tug. In your mind's eye, you imagine all the colours inside that box: gold, silver, red, green . . . But maybe that's just the oxygen deprivation talking. You're sure you're almost out of air. Just get that box open, get more air, and start collecting your well-earned booty!

With one last muster of strength, you fling the lid of the chest open. It swings easily, and you take a look inside to see—

"GAAARRGLE!" you scream, as the last of your air escapes your lungs. Octopus! Big octopus!

It must have been living in the box this whole time. No wonder all that gold had spilled out. You turn and race to the surface, but you feel a thick tentacle coil around one of your legs, then the other. A third tentacle grabs hold of your waist, pulling you down.

You try to scream, but with nothing left in your lungs, you just swallow gulps of salty, cold sea water.

Down you go, and as the octopus tightens its grip, everything grows dark.

THE END.

To try again, go back to page 22.

03:58

lecch! You've been through enough today without having to lug a hundreds-year-old hand around with you. In fact, who's to say you even need to go back to that lighthouse at all? Once you have the treasure, you can go to the mainland and find your parents. You're holding all the cards now.

You finish filling your pockets. It's a shame they're not bigger because there's still a bit of treasure left, and you're not going to be able to drag that chest back through Death's Swamp by yourself. But that's fine—you know the secret path and can come back with your mom and dad.

You start to make your way to the boat. That means splashing back into the swamp and keeping your eyes peeled for those snakes. *Urgh. Why did it have to be snakes?*

Doesn't matter. You just stay focused on your new-found riches, and that's enough to push you forward. Except...

You keep hearing *something* splashing through the muck with you. At first you pass it off as the snakes, until...

You hear it again and whip around, spilling some

of the coins into the murky waters. "Dang!"

You double your speed. A few more coins fall into the water as you push ahead. You watch them disappear under the surface. *Careful*, you tell yourself. *Walk quickly but carefully.*

You look ahead and see the other edge of the swamp. It's just a few metres away. Just a few more steps—

SPLASH!

Something grabs your leg.

"GAH!" you scream, and a whole bunch of the treasure flings out of your pockets, scattering into the swamp.

You whirl around, only to see—

THE HAND!

There it is, clutching your ankle in a viselike grip. It pulls you back, deeper and deeper into the swamp.

You try to scream and just end up gagging on the swamp water. You try feverishly to pull the hand off you, but it only pulls you in deeper.

The last thing you see as you're dragged under completely is that disgusting hand giving you a final thumbs-up.

THE END.

To try again, go back to page 136.

lecch! That hand is super gross, but a promise is a promise, even if it's to a ghost. You fill your pockets with as many jewels and coins as you're able. You know where the treasure is located; you can always come back here later. For now, it's time to make good on your promise, then find your parents.

You're not sure where to put the hand, so you place it on your shoulder. Rather creepily, the finger bones clench your shirt, keeping the hand in place. "Urgh." You shudder, but keep your mind focused on getting through the swamp and back to the mainland.

You've nearly reached the other side of the swamp when Feared Beard suddenly materializes before you.

You scream and jump, falling into the water.

"Arrr." Feared Beard smiles. "You found the secret path! And I see you made good on yer promise!" He eyes the hand.

"I keep my word," you tell the ghost. "What are you even doing here?"

"I don't know how ye'll be driving that thar boat home without *this*." Feared Beard dangles the key to the men's boat from his ghostly hook.

"Right! The key! Thanks!"

You think about this. "How did you even pick that up?"

"Ghost power!" Feared Beard says.

"And, come to think of it, how did you get all the way here?"

"*Ultra* ghost power!" Feared Beard smiles.

"So why didn't you just transport yourself here and get your hand yourself?"

Feared Beard waves you off. "You ask too many questions."

Then he floats past you, towards the boat still anchored nearby. "Come. The treasure and your parents await! Along with much stirring conversation. Oh, we're going to be good friends, you and I."

"What do you mean?"

"Well, now that me treasure's been found, I'll be needing a new place to haunt. Looks like we'll be friends for some time yet!"

You roll your eyes. Having a tagalong ghost pirate isn't your idea of a good time, but that's just what you've got with your new not-quite-best friend. Lots and lots of time.

00:00

You survived! There are eleven other ways to escape the danger—try to find them all!

You're not tangling with these guys. You make a move for the stairs beside you. Up you go, and when you reach the top, you're caught by a blast of sea air. The lens rotates around the lighthouse, sending a beam of intense light to the nearby surroundings. You grab hold of the rusted railing along the edge of the tower. It seems precarious, and it's a long drop to the ground. There's no way you'd survive trying to scale the wall down.

"Come on, kid. You're wasting your time up there," one of the men says, as the three of them head up after you.

You shake your head. "You're not taking me."

"What choice do you have? There's only one way down," he says. He's standing by the open stairwell. The others move in opposite directions, blocking you in from either end.

You look around, and then you look dead ahead at the light. Or rather, *below* it. There's that long pole attached to the lens. You could jump to it. Slide down. And get past these guys.

You shrug. *I'll try my luck*, you think.

And you jump.

You sail through the air, arms outstretched. For a second you worry this was a bad idea.

And then you connect with the pole and grip it tightly. "HA!" you bellow.

You begin to slide down the pole to safety. "Looks like luck is on my side after all!"

But as you look down, you realize you're sliding really fast. And you forgot about that big metal gear at the bottom of the pole.

"Oh," you say.

You're going to have to time this right. But you're sliding really, really fast.

You let go of the pole, and once again you're flying through the air.

And then the set of gears comes rushing at you.

CRUNCH.

THE END.

To try again, go back to page 134.

The men advance towards you. You've got only one shot at this, so you wait until they're within range and—

"COWABUNGA!" you shout at the top of your lungs. Then you rush them at full speed. Sure enough, they're not expecting your reverse tactic and dodge out of your way as you barrel through them and down the stairwell.

Racing away from them is your plan, except you don't do it so gracefully. Literally two steps in, you trip and fall. Down the steps you tumble, flipping and bumping the whole way.

"Gah!"

"Ack!"

"Yee-ouch!"

"Mama!"

By the time you lie splayed on the floor below, you're not sure if you're still in one piece or the human equivalent of mashed potatoes. Groggily you lift your head and arms, then move your legs. Everything seems to be working.

At the top of the lighthouse, three large heads look down at you. Did they actually just stand there and watch you fall? They clap their hands, clearly impressed at your little show. And then they rush down after you.

You bolt upright. Pain flares through your body, but no matter. You have a head start. Then you realize why they're moving so quickly. Is it to capture you, or to prevent you from getting to their boat? That gets you to your feet and running through the door of the lighthouse.

Your head spins as you manoeuvre over the rocks, making your way to the shoreline. You quickly look over your shoulder. There they are. But *you're* closer to the boat. You splash towards it, jump on board, and dash to the controls. Then you realize they would never be so careless as to leave the key in the ignition, and your heart sinks.

Except . . .

You give it a turn. The boat's engine roars to life as the men race towards you.

One of them slaps his head. "Gak! The key!"

"THANKS A BUNCH!" you shout.

The three men are nearly at the hull when you crank the steering wheel and angle the boat towards the open ocean before speeding away. Luck's on your side today. You've got the map, the boat and now the upper hand.

00:00

You survived! There are eleven other ways to escape the danger—try to find them all!

SPLASH!

It's the second time you've ended up in the Atlantic today, and it's no less awful. You're cold, again, but for now you're safe. Even the airplane seems to have moved away. Probably because of the fog.

And that's just what you need. The fog will be the perfect cover to separate yourself from Erin. You begin to paddle like mad, hoping all those swimming lessons will come in handy.

Behind you, Erin revs the engine. You turn around to see she's hit the throttle and is driving the boat. Right. At. You.

You throw your hands up to wave her away and inadvertently toss the map out of reach. The waves push it farther and farther away, towards a huge boulder poking out of the water. Erin's boat bears down on you.

You could leave it and swim to the island, perhaps. But without that map, do you even stand a chance? You could also try to lie low on the boulder, hoping you lose Erin in the fog, then double back for the map.

If you swim to the boulder, turn to page 39.
If you swim to the island, turn to page 121.

If someone else is after the treasure, you're going to need an ally. Erin might be up to something, but right now she's your only option.

For a second, you both watch as the seaplane flies closer.

"What the—?" you start.

VOOM!

The plane dive-bombs you, its thick landing floats nearly clipping the top of the speedboat.

You duck for cover as the heavy floats connect briefly with the ocean, sending up a huge spray of water. Then the plane takes to the air. It banks, then turns to make another run at you.

You eye the plane as it starts its second attack.

"Come on," you say. "We can lose them in the fog."

"There's no visibility. We'll crash and get stranded."

"We're sitting ducks here," you snap.

The roar of the plane is deafening. It's coming at you, fast.

Enough is enough. You grab the wheel and hit the throttle.

The engine roars and you're nearly thrown off the boat. But you grip the steering wheel and yank it hard to the right, toppling Erin in the process.

The plane just misses the boat.

Erin struggles to her feet and over to you, but you give the wheel another sharp turn and she's thrown the other way. "Sorry," you shout, "but we don't have time to play around."

"You fool!" she yells. "You don't even know how to steer this thing!"

You turn the boat in circles, sending water flying in every direction. It's true—this is not exactly your forte, but it's working.

You straighten the boat out and aim it right for the fog.

Erin tries to grab the wheel. "You're out of control!" she shouts. "You're going to kill us!"

Suddenly, you disappear into the fog. But as you look over your shoulder, you see the plane is still right on your tail.

Erin screams, and you immediately know why— you're racing straight towards the rocky edge of the island.

There's barely time to react. You crank the throttle and prepare to make another sharp turn.

If you steer to the left, turn to page 131.
If you steer to the right, turn to page 132.

You need to get out of the ocean as fast as you can, and boats clearly are not on your side today. Neither is water, since all you can think about are the creatures lurking in the frigid depths, waiting to make a meal out of you.

And that's what gives you the extra push you need to make your way to the nearby island. You try to clear thoughts of sea creatures and tour boats from your head. You focus on taking deep breaths and swimming like mad towards the lighthouse.

Soon your feet touch something solid. You let out a yelp, wondering if it's some kind of whale or shark, but then you feel the crunch of small rocks. You're finally out of the deep water.

As you wade to shore, you gaze up at the lighthouse. Now that you're closer, you can see it's an old, derelict structure. It's crumbling in places, and bits of concrete and rock from its walls are mixed in among the island's dark, jagged boulders and a surprisingly large number of fish skeletons.

But at least you're safe!

You turn back around, and—

"Oh no!" you whisper.

A boat emblazoned with *Captain John Longsilver's Fishing Tours* is pulling up to the island. It looks like there's three big men on the deck. They must have seen you in the water and followed you here. If they catch you, it's game over.

There's no way you'll be able to swim somewhere else without them spotting you. You're going to have to find a place to hide, and quick! The lighthouse looks like it might collapse any minute, but it must have a million nooks and crannies inside. Maybe you can lie low there. Then again, the lighthouse looks like it might collapse any minute . . .

If you go into the lighthouse, turn to page 134.

If you hide among the rocks outside, turn to page 136.

You turn and swim towards the larger object. As you get closer, you quickly understand: it's a massive shipwreck. This has got to be where those divers are, and maybe where the real treasure is. You'll definitely find the answers you seek here.

But it also raises more questions. This boat is unlike anything you've seen before. For one thing, it's ancient. At first you wonder if it's made of old planks of wood, but even that throws you. The hull is composed of a material you can't place. Or maybe it just looks that way from years of sitting at the bottom of the ocean. But as you pass closer, you notice that the texture of the ship's planks seems more like . . . coral?

Could there actually be a ship made of coral?

You shake your head. That's impossible. Coral is a living thing. It isn't grown in long chunks to be put onto the bottoms of boats. It must have just grown on top of the boat over all these years. Although . . . there's no coral anywhere else on this sea floor.

Curiosity pulls you farther along the edge of the boat.

Is this where the divers are?

You strain to see if there are any air bubbles coming

from the wreck, but there's no sign of human life inside the boat. Where else would they be?

Then, as you cross the hull, you see it: a large, gaping hole in the bottom of the boat. What had it crashed into?

You're not sure about that, but you know it's the easiest way into the wreck.

Turn to page 93.

Is all that glitters gold? It's worth a shot. You swim towards the shining objects and are soon rewarded with a small pile of coins on the sea floor below you. *A-ha!* So there *is* a treasure after all!

You grab a couple of coins, then bring them closer to your mask and try to get a look at their surface. They're old and irregular, like they were moulded by hand. You don't recognize the writing on the back; even the letters are foreign to you. And the image, which shows a half-person, half-fish figure, stumps you. *Merman? Who puts that on a coin?*

Wherever these coins are from, you're pretty sure they're made of gold. And ancient. And worth a lot!

Is this what your parents wanted you to find?

You try to remember, but your mind is still blank. Maybe if you can find the rest of this treasure, you'll also find the answers you seek.

Speaking of answers, is this what the divers from the boat are looking for? And where exactly are they, anyway?

You search the murky waters around you. If there are a few coins here, there must be more somewhere else. If the divers haven't already found them, that is.

You drop one of the coins to mark your place and swim farther ahead.

You move several metres through the water, then catch sight of a chasm in the rocky bottom. You try to look down the sloping rock wall, but it just disappears into nothing.

You feel around on your vest for the small light you know is there, then aim its beam into the abyss. The light is quickly swallowed up by a seemingly impenetrable darkness. *How deep does this thing go?*

You've heard of the Mariana Trench—the deepest spot on earth—but that's in the middle of the Pacific Ocean, and you're just off the Atlantic coast of Canada. There's nothing here that should go that deep.

Could the divers have tried to swim into it?

You keep swimming alongside the edge of the chasm, and then you spot it—mostly hidden and almost the exact colour of the rocky slope itself. It's a chest!

That's got to be a treasure chest, right?

Hovering above it, you feel the currents sweeping you over the edge of the chasm, so you fight them and swim back to the other side.

But that chest doesn't have the ability to swim or to propel itself. It begins to teeter unsteadily over the edge of the abyss.

If it falls, the treasure will be lost forever. And no treasure means you risk never finding your parents.

Of course, you have no idea what's actually in that chest. Trying to get the chest right now might be way too much to risk for a pile of old wood. Maybe you're meant to find something else down here. Something that doesn't involve a giant hole to nowhere.

If you grab hold of the chest, turn to page 91.

If you leave the chest and swim back to explore the other object you spotted, turn to page 26.

You hate to be rude to these Atlanteans. After all, you're probably the first human who's been down here in eons.

You are quickly seated between two elderly Atlanteans. You watch them take fork-sized tridents and politely twirl their noodles. Only they're not noodles—they're the still-wriggling tentacles of some kind of octopus. Only it's not an octopus, because judging by the mass of squirming limbs, this creature has at least thirty tentacles.

You pick up your mini trident and stare at your plate. Your appetite has just gone out the window.

"Do you not like raw hurgledsnort?" the man to your left asks you.

You look at him blankly.

"Oh, hurgledsnort is just divine," the woman on your right chimes in.

"Uh, sure," you say. You realize that all of the Atlanteans are looking at you.

Great. You've got to see this through to the end now.

With a shaky hand, you jab the end of your trident into the middle of the plate. The tentacles flop and wave uncontrollably. But you're not going to give up. You do your best to twirl a bunch of them onto your trident and bring it close to your face. You close your eyes, open your mouth, pop it in, and—

"Hey," you say, through a mouthful of hurgledsnort. "This is delicious!"

"Indeed," the woman says.

Without another word, you twirl more of the hurgledsnort onto your trident and take a big bite. Sure, it's raw and cold, but the taste is like nothing you've ever experienced. You chew and swallow, amazed at the palate of flavour, until—

Something's not right. Is the hurgledsnort trying to wriggle out of your throat?

No, it's not that. Your hands start to shake.

You drop your trident. The plate and the hurgledsnort clatter to the floor. You try to get up, but your legs are weak.

CRASH! You fall to the ground. The room spins around you. Something's wrong with the hurgledsnort. Maybe not for those Atlanteans, but for you. Bad idea to have dinner in a strange undersea city, with strange undersea people, eating strange undersea delicacies.

You open your mouth, gasp, and give your last burp.

At least it's a tasty one.

THE END.
To try again, go back to page 47.

"Sure thing," you start. "I'll eat . . . back on the surface!"

Before the Atlanteans can react, you run out of the dining hall. Yup, your submersible is toast, but these guys must have some kind of gear to get to the surface.

In fact, as you run down the street, between buildings made of coral, you see some of the Atlanteans literally floating above you in blobs of goo. It looks like the same material the wall of the city is made of—translucent with a bioluminescent glow.

You watch as one of the Atlanteans brings a blob down to the ground not far from you. You tear off after it. The pilot literally steps out of the blob, its wobbly wall allowing her to pass through. She wanders off without giving you a second glance.

You, meanwhile, run at full tilt, skidding to a halt beside the strange, blobby vehicle.

"Okay," you say. "Here goes nothing." You take a deep breath and try to slide inside. But instead of gliding through the membrane, your body just slaps against the wet exterior and you get a mouthful of seaweedy slime.

"Yecch!" you blurt, before falling backwards and landing firmly on your butt.

The Atlantean who escorted you into the dining hall catches up to you and pulls you to your feet. "It doesn't work that way," he says. "We don't build the pods. We simply learn to control the material that forms our city. There is much you have to learn about our ways. And much you can teach us about the world above. Now, you see, you *must* stay."

"But . . ." You try to think of an excuse to get back to the surface. Even if you could, would they let you? "But what about my family?"

"Oh, don't worry. We will find you a new one here. But first, you must come back to feast on the delicious tentacle soup of the hurgledsnort."

"The WHAT?" you say, as you are led back to the dining hall.

It's time to end your quest for treasure and begin your new life as a citizen of the lost city of Atlantis. But there's no way you're ever going to try a bite of hurgledsnort . . .

00:00

You survived! There are eleven other ways to escape the danger— try to find them all!

You came here for the treasure, and you're not going to let a broken compass stop you. You lead the way, carefully manoeuvring across the rugged landscape. After what feels like an eternity, you see something cutting through the fog up ahead.

It's a ship, but it's like no ship you've ever seen. The thing is a hulking, ancient galleon—the kind of boat you'd expect old-fashioned pirates to be sailing. But how did it get *here*, in the middle of land? As you step towards it, you see the silhouettes of two more boats beyond it. One looks like a modern sailing ship. The other resembles an ancient canoe.

You look back down at your compass and gasp. The needle is spinning wildly.

"I think we should try somewhere else," you say. "This place gives me the creeps."

Erin nods, and you go back the way you came. After a little while, you see a shape through the fog.

"What the—" Erin starts. You're back at the ship graveyard.

"We must have gotten turned around," you say. "Let's try again."

This time you're careful to walk in the exact opposite

direction of the ship, even though the compass is still no help. Finally, you see a dark outline up ahead. You've made it back to Erin's boat! The fog clears a little and—

"Oh no," you whisper. Once again, the pirate ship looms in front of you.

"Erin," you say. You feel her hand clasp around your arm.

Erin looks grim. "I've heard rumours about this place," she says. "I just didn't believe it actually existed. According to the stories, anyone who ends up here can never leave."

You wonder if she might be right, and see the compass has started spinning in the other direction. You sigh as you look back at the map, and then it hits you.

These other ships must have been looking for the treasure too. You finally notice that shovels litter the ground, and there are holes dug out everywhere in the rocky terrain.

"Well," you say, "if we're stuck here, we might as well start digging."

You pick up one of the shovels, and Erin does the same.

Good thing there are two of you for the job.

THE END.

To try again, go back to page 21.

01:43

"**S**omething's not right," you tell Erin. "That compass is messed up, this island feels like a death trap and there's something very wrong with this fog. Let's try one of the other spots on the map."

For once, Erin agrees with you. She digs into her pocket and pulls out the key for the boat. "Let's go."

No sooner does she hold it up than the key drops from her hand.

In an instant, it slips through a crack in the rocks and is gone.

You and Erin stand there, dumbfounded. "Impossible," Erin says.

She bends down to pull at the rocks on the ground and succeeds only in cutting her fingers. You can see that the crevice is deeper than either of you would ever be able to reach.

You look over your shoulder. "We've still got your boat, right?"

"And no way to drive it."

"We could radio for help," you try.

She shakes her head. "I haven't got one. My boat is untraceable."

"So what do we do now?"

Erin looks around at the desolate surroundings. "Let's see. No plants, really. No fresh water. And a boat with no key."

"But people will be looking for us, right?"

"Sure," Erin says, staring out to sea. You look in her direction and watch as the fog slowly rolls in, shrouding the two of you in its thick white haze.

THE END.

To try again, go back to page 21.

You cut through the choppy waters in just enough time to pull yourself onto the boulder before Erin speeds past. You crouch, waiting for her to take another pass at you, but you're knocked off your feet as the ground below you shakes. *What's going on?* you wonder.

Either the island around you is moving or . . . you are! You look down at the strangely organic surface of the boulder.

Then, *POOF!*

A huge geyser shoots into the air just centimetres ahead of you. You catch a whiff of a thick, animal stink, and the ground shifts again. Then you see it. The huge flukes of a massive tail lift out of the water and slap the surface. You whirl around to see the water briefly being breached by the head of an enormous whale. A whale moving far away from the island.

Okay, so you're not going to get to the treasure anytime soon. You're not even sure where it is you're going. Only one thing's certain—you're about to have a whale of a tale to tell.

THE END.

To try again, go back to page 96.

14:56

You didn't wake up this morning thinking it was going to come down to a battle of claw vs. tentacle, but that's just how it goes.

You reach your hands into little compartments on either side of the submersible's front end. Your fists close around controls that move the arm-like protrusions with metal claws fixed to their ends. They were probably meant for gripping and moving things; today they're going to save your life.

You have no time to practise, though. The creature hurls itself at the submersible, throwing you back against the rocks.

You hear a loud *CLANG* and a *HISS*, then feel a small jet of water on your back.

Yikes! How long will it take for the submersible to fill with water? You don't want to wait around to find out.

You activate the controls, pulling away from the tentacle monster and swivelling around. This time, *you're* going to be the one to attack. You try to get the sub to ramming speed, but the monster is racing towards you. It flashes a blinding beam of light at you. You're forced to close your eyes. As you do, you instinctively clench the controls.

You feel a huge thud as the creature smashes against the sub, then you hear what can only be described as a monstrous cry.

Now it's moving away from you, flailing its tentacles wildly. A weird translucent jelly pours out of two wounds. A-ha! You can take this thing.

But the submersible is quickly filling with water. A crack appears on your windshield.

You don't have time to waste. You push the submersible ahead at full throttle, right towards the creature. It turns towards you—

WHAM!

The sub crashes into it. You reach forward with the claw. The water in the cab is making it difficult to manoeuvre. You try to snap the claw shut on one of the creature's tentacles, and it howls with rage when you miss.

Then you jab the other claw into the creature's gelatinous side.

The water is up to your chest now. You've got to get out of here.

You give it one final jab, then aim the sub towards the surface. You just need to get there before the submersible fills.

Looking down, you see the creature's dark form hovering in the distance. It's not going to chase you. But will you run out of air before you reach the surface?

Water fills the sub, past your neck, your chin, your mouth, your nose—

You hold your breath.

Please, please . . . just a few metres more.

Your lungs feel like they're going to burst, when—

SPLASH! The sub breaks the surface. You're almost out of air when you hit the *EMERGENCY RELEASE* button on the controls.

POW! The domed lid pops off the sub, and you lift your head out of the water, gasping for breath.

When you've managed to breathe normally again, you look over to the dive boat. You've only just begun to scratch the surface of the treasure map's mysteries. But you've got a boat and a radio, and you're pretty sure you know where the treasure is.

Now you just need to find your parents . . .

00:00

You survived! There are eleven other ways to escape the danger—try to find them all!

The creature was startled by the camera's flash. Maybe you can do a solid for the scientific community *and* save your skin.

You turn around, aiming the submersible's camera right at the monster. You're not sure where its eyes are, but it's definitely sensitive to light—which probably explains why it came from the abyss.

"Say cheese!" you chirp from inside the sub, and then—

FLASH! FLASH! FLASH!

You set off several bursts of light as you take a bunch of pictures.

It lets out a roar that passes from the water, through the solid Plexiglas dome, to your ears. *Urgh, what a sound!* You fire off another round of flashes, then clamp your hands to your ears to block out the thing's horrid wails.

But instead of screaming this time, the creature whips around and shoots one of its tentacles right at the sub.

You pull your hands off your ears, but you're not fast enough to reach the controls. Two tentacles grab some of the mechanical bits on the outside of the sub, pulling it towards the creature's open mouth.

You scream as the creature's beak rushes towards you—

CRUNCH!

It bites down hard on the outer edge of the submersible.

You try to throw the sub into reverse, but this thing's *way* stronger than your motors.

Still, the creature seems to have bitten off more than it can chew. It spits you out, then flings the sub towards the edge of the chasm.

"Phew!" you say, pleased you're not exactly meal material—

SMASH!

The sub is thrown against the wall of the chasm with such force that you hear something above you crunch.

A red warning light begins to flash.

That's not good.

You try to rev the engines and pilot yourself out of the abyss, but the controls won't respond. The motor is shot!

"No, no, no!"

You look around and see the creature eerily pass over top of you. It knocks over the nearby chest, which plummets into the darkness below.

And, you realize, you're plummeting with it.

Turn to page 74.

The good news is that Erin is about as light on her feet as a rhinoceros on roller skates. Like you, she keeps stumbling into stuff, except she's cursing up a storm while she's at it.

You don't have the luxury of letting out your frustrations as you bump around the island. Any big noise and you'll give yourself away. In fact, when you trip and nearly land face first on the rocks, you're forced to bite your lip so hard you draw blood.

The fog is too thick to gauge which direction you and Erin are moving in. Most likely, you're heading in circles. Although maybe not, because Erin suddenly lets out a big "A-ha!"

She doesn't say much after that, so you creep as close as you can. Erin has the map opened up in her hands. Her attention is directed somewhere below. Has she spotted the treasure?

She definitely hasn't spotted you.

That leaves you with a few opportunities. Either way, it's time to make your presence known.

If you tackle Erin to get the map, turn to page 71.

If you offer to help Erin look for the treasure, turn to page 72.

It's a good thing your mom made you take those scuba lessons before your last family vacation. Soon enough you're sporting an oxygen tank, a weight belt, a buoyancy vest and a pair of flippers.

Then you put a regulator in your mouth and jump into the water with a big splash.

Letting the air out of your vest, you slowly make your descent. The deeper you go, the darker it gets.

Even so, you notice a mixture of sand, rock and the odd bit of kelp swaying in the current as you approach the seabed. Now that you're down here, it's time to explore. You start swimming through the cool sea water and quickly spot something large and dark looming up ahead. Whatever it is, it has a curved, definite shape like it was made by people.

You're beginning to move closer when the remaining sunlight illuminates something shiny and golden not far from you.

If you explore the larger object, turn to page 26.

If you investigate what's reflecting in the light, turn to page 28.

The submersible is just large enough to fit a person. It has a domed window and two claw-like protrusions at the front and a pair of motors at the back. Seeing as there's nobody on the boat to tell you *not* to take the submersible, you climb inside and switch on the controls.

It looked like a complicated piece of machinery, but you seem to be able to operate the controls easily enough. You're even able to manipulate the one that releases the submersible, and—

SPLASH!

It plunges into the ocean, your field of vision quickly filling with a deep-blue hue.

You start to steer the submersible deeper. Your foggy memory and the intrigue of the unknown keep pushing you forward—that, and the knowledge that there may be a treasure somewhere down here.

As you descend, the sunlight gets fainter and fainter. You're probably reaching the point where the pressures of the deep would be too much for regular divers. But the ocean keeps dropping and you haven't seen any signs of human life. You flick on the submersible's headlamps, which illuminate the soupy sea water ahead of you.

Down you go, until the sea floor looms into view.

You train the headlamps on the ground ahead of you, slowly cruising along the ocean floor.

Soon enough, the rocky sea floor drops away as you pass over a chasm. You aim the light beam into it, and even though these headlamps are powerful, they're totally swallowed by the chasm's seemingly impenetrable depths.

Weird, you think.

Weirder still—as you move across the chasm, you see something teetering near the edge.

It's an old wooden chest!

A *treasure chest*?

You pilot the submersible closer. *Impossible!* This thing is perched so close to the edge, it's almost like someone put it there on purpose. What if this is a trap?

Nevertheless, if this is the treasure that's marked on the map, it might be worth the risk.

If you try to open the chest, turn to page 113.

If you explore a bit first, turn to page 115.

You'd rather know sooner than later if there's someone else here, so you decide to start with the hut.

Once you get close to it, you can see it's not exactly a hut. It's actually about as big as a decent-sized house, just one that's taken a beating from the wind and sea. You hang on to the storm shutter flapping against the closest window and try to peer inside, but the interior of the place is dark. Hadn't there been a light on earlier? You're sure it was lit enough for you to see something moving inside.

You decide there's only one way to find out what's up with this "hut." You head to the front door, take a deep breath, and carefully twist the knob. The door is unlocked, and as you push it open, it makes a heavy, foreboding creak.

You feel around for a light switch, and your fingers land on one beside the door. You flick it on, but you're not prepared for what you find: a large laboratory fills the main floor of the house. Amazingly, the house's interior does not match the dilapidated exterior. The walls are a sterile white, and they're lined with desks holding all manner of expensive-looking equipment: bubbling beakers, vials of liquid, brand-new computers and a strange array of sea creatures in fish tanks.

The place also appears to be completely deserted, so you carefully move over to a row of aquariums to take a closer look. Wow—there are some pretty big lobsters in one of the larger tanks. You've never seen anything like that in the grocery store.

The next tank houses oysters, shrimp and eels—all of them much larger than anything in nature.

Beyond the aquariums is a large cylindrical vat. A ladder has been positioned alongside it, and you take a few steps up to see what's inside.

Once you're looking into the container, you can't believe what you catch a whiff of.

"Chowder?" you say. At least, that's what you're smelling. You'd know that salty smell of cooking seafood anywhere. As you look down at the briny brew, you are tempted to grab a sip of it.

It's not that it looks that delicious—it's a little too watery for your liking—but there's something about the smell. Something hypnotic, even. You keep sniffing at it. It's like the chowder is saying *drink me*.

"Yes," you say to yourself, and begin to reach a hand down to scoop some of it up.

"I wouldn't do that if I were you," says a voice behind you.

You turn to see a woman entering the room. She's

wearing a white lab coat and staring at you. "I see you've made it here in one piece."

"What do you mean?" you say. She doesn't look surprised to see you. Does she know you? You definitely can't place her. But your memory is still fuzzy, and your stomach is growling. Maybe your mind will be a little sharper if you eat something.

Something like that chowder, right?

That delicious-smelling chowder . . .

If you listen to the scientist, turn to page 108.
If you try the chowder, turn to page 111.

The X is down by the water, so that's where you need to focus your attention. Whatever's going on with the hut can wait.

You keep moving towards the edge of the peninsula. It's not as easy as it seems, though. The closer you get to the water, the slicker the rocks get, and you find yourself slipping and falling on more than one occasion. You also keep catching sight of something at the water's edge.

Then, over the roar of waves pounding against the rocks, you start to hear a loud clicking and clacking.

You can't see much beyond the rock face in front of you, but as you round it, you're—

CLICK! CLACK! CLICK!

"Gak!" you scream, falling back on your butt, hard. Then you realize you're staring at two massive lobsters.

Not just massive—HUMAN SIZED.

You sit there, aghast at the sight. How on earth could lobsters ever become so big? And what are they doing *on land*?

More importantly, you realize they must be what you've been seeing and hearing this whole time. And as they raise their massive claws—which look like they could crush you as easily as you might squash a pop can with your foot—you're sure they have the upper hand. Er, claw.

You back up, looking for something to defend yourself with. All around you are rocks and boulders, but not much else. You're not sure you can fight them off with a few rocks. Maybe you should make a run for it instead.

If you stay and fight the lobsters, turn to page 88.
If you run away, turn to page 89.

You're better off hiding than gasping up any more stairs. You push into the room and feel around. Sure enough, there's another switch here. When you flick it on, a string of lights along the ceiling illuminates a large metal object. Pipes jut out of it at all kinds of angles, and you see a row of dials, along with other valves and clutches. This must be some kind of generator, but not for the puny lights overheard. And then you notice a label on one of the dials: *FOGHORN*.

Footsteps and voices echo up the stairs. They're already inside. You're far enough up the stairs that they can't see you or the lights in the room, but you don't have much time.

You look around and spot a large breaker beside a big drum that smells like diesel. Maybe this is the *ON* switch? You give it a hefty push. Sure enough, the machine starts squeaking to life. Metal grinding against metal sets your teeth on edge, and it's likely you've just attracted even more attention.

You track the different parts of the machinery until you see a long chain dangling from one of the valves above your head. The chain isn't attached to the generator, and you realize it must go directly to the foghorn.

There were boats out on the water. None by the lighthouse, but foghorns can be heard for kilometres, can't they?

It doesn't look like this thing has been used for years, so any sound coming from it will attract attention from people other than the men, which is exactly what you need.

The question is, can you remember the code for SOS? You're not sure, so maybe you should try one big long blast instead.

If you send out an SOS blast, turn to page 122.
If you make one long blast, turn to page 129.

You don't care how tired you are, you're getting as far away from these guys as you can. You race up the spiral staircase to the top of the lighthouse, taking the steps two at a time. Below, the door squeals open. A shaft of light punches through the dim entryway, and you see three silhouettes push into the bottom of the lighthouse.

They look around the main level for a moment, then crane their heads up. You duck against the wall. Maybe they didn't see you, but even so, it doesn't matter. You push away from the wall and bolt up the stairs. The men's shouts push you farther, faster, despite you feeling more exhausted with every step. You're close to the top now, and you can see the lighthouse's service room.

You fling open the door and find giant metal gears. That's what the switch downstairs must have activated! Sure enough, you see the lens rotating above you, connected to the gears by a long pole.

You close the door behind you and search for a place to hide. But all you find is a staircase leading to an upper deck beside the lens.

Suddenly, the men fling the door open and enter

the service room. You back up so that the large gear is between you and them.

"Okay, kid," one says. "Enough's enough. We'll get you to your parents, and then we can get you home. Once we have the map, of course."

You instinctively pat your shirt to ensure the map's still there. Then you raise the flare gun and point it right at the men's feet. If you can give them a good, solid scare, you might be able to bolt past them.

They raise their hands defensively. "Whoa, whoa," the apparent leader says. "Easy there. Let's not get ahead of ourselves."

"Oh, I'm definitely ahead of myself," you say, and squeeze the trigger, bracing for a loud bang and flash of light.

Instead, the flare fizzles out and lands with a dull *clunk*.

"Erm," you say, nervously.

The men lower their hands and narrow their eyes.

You realize you're almost out of options and need to make a split-second decision: Do you run towards them or away from them?

If you run away, turn to page 17.
If you run at the kidnappers, turn to page 19.

There's something about Feared Beard's warning that stops you. After all, if he's telling you not to go splashing through the water, maybe it's for good reason!

So you turn back around, moving through the fog and keeping low to the ground.

"Good thinking," Feared Beard tells you. "If you keep a low profile, they'll never find you."

"Will you quiet down," you whisper angrily.

"Oh, right. My mistake. You're trying to stay inconspicuous."

You move along the misty shoreline, trying to listen for Captain John's crew over the constant babble of Feared Beard.

Suddenly, a massive hand clamps down on your shoulder. You look up to see one of the men towering over you. He has a decidedly malicious glint in his eye.

"Where's the map, kid?" he asks, as the others approach.

Before you can tell him you don't know what he's talking about, a second man snatches the map right out of your shirt.

"Perfect," says the one still holding you. "May as

well take the kid with us. We might need someone to test for booby traps."

"Me? But I don't know anything about booby traps."

"You don't have to," he replies. "Now get going."

"Great," you snap, looking around for the ghost. "You were all interested in haunting me, Feared Beard, but what about these guys?"

One of the men nudges another in the ribs. "See? The kid knows all about Feared Beard's treasure."

"This is *Feared Beard's treasure*?" you ask. Maybe you should have listened a little more closely to all his babbling.

"You know what we're after," the man holding you says. Then they force you down the shore towards their boat.

Turn to page 10.

You're almost out of air as it is, so you decide to leave the chest for now. You scramble to grab as many of the scattered coins as you can, then kick your legs hard to propel yourself upward.

Your head breaks the surface of the water and you gasp for fresh air, although you're mostly taking in whiffs of the seaplane's smoky wreckage.

You turn your attention to Erin and the pilot, who are both in the water. You're not sure which one to side with. Then it hits you: they're not fighting.

It's Erin! She's *helping* the pilot. Hang on a second. Wasn't she planning on leaving him hanging?

You swim over to Erin and the pilot, who is struggling to stay afloat.

"What's going on?" you ask. "You told me—"

"Changed my mind," Erin says, almost out of breath. "You were right. We can't leave him there. Come and help me pull him to the boat."

You grab one arm, and Erin grabs the other. Together you make your way back to Erin's boat. Erin pulls herself up, and you push the pilot towards her. Soon the three of you lie exhausted and panting for air, but safely back on board.

The pilot looks at you and Erin. "You saved my life."

You shrug. "Good thing you didn't hit us with your plane."

"Right," the pilot says, looking sheepish. "I didn't realize it was a couple of kids that I was sent after."

Erin scowls. "Who are you calling a kid?"

"Look," you say. "I know where the treasure is. All I want is my parents. After that, the two of you are welcome to split it any way you like." You decide not to mention the gold coins you already took.

Erin and the pilot look at you, and then at each other. Instinctively, you back away from them.

"Easy, easy," the pilot says, and reaches a hand out. Erin shakes it. "So, we're agreed? We split the treasure, and we'll get you to your parents."

Erin and the pilot look to you as if you're the final say in all of this.

Actually, as it turns out, you're the only one who knows where the treasure is, so you *are*.

00:00

You survived! There are eleven other ways to escape the danger— try to find them all!

aybe you're hallucinating this ghost, or maybe not. But you have nothing to hide from Feared Beard, so you explain everything that's happened today. At least you try to, but Feared Beard stops you when he hears . . .

"The map!" he exclaims. "You've found it?"

"It's right here," you say, pulling it out of your shirt.

Feared Beard's eyes grow wide. He reaches out to grab it from you, but his hand passes right through your body. "Whoops," he says.

You shiver and unroll the map. "You know about this?"

"Of course I do," he says. "I made that map."

"What are you talking about?"

"Look," he says, pointing to the edge of the map that shows a small stretch of land and a lighthouse symbol. "Thar be this lighthouse, right here. Those double-crossing, no-good scallywag partners of mine buried most of me here."

"*Most* of you?"

"Me left hand's on that island, THERE," he says, jabbing his hook at one of the islands on the map. "Right with me treasure."

You shake your head in disbelief. "I can't get you your

treasure," you stammer. "I've got to rescue my parents."

Feared Beard shrugs. "Keep the treasure," he says. "All I want is me hand. Do we have a deal?"

"You want me to dig up your left hand?"

"Trust me. It's buried right there with the treasure. Except . . ." Feared Beard stops, thinking. "Except, you'd better watch out for the booby traps."

"Booby traps?"

"Yes, that's right. Booby traps! Deadly ones too! Just in case anyone ever tried to get to the treasure without me. I've got tons of them about."

"So, your map is just going to lead me to near-certain doom?"

Feared Beard shakes his head. "Hold that map up to me face."

"Why?"

"Trust me."

You're about to tell Feared Beard that you don't trust any stranger, let alone strange ghosts, let alone strange pirate ghosts. And then you decide to just go with it.

You hold the map towards him.

"Other way," he says. "Turn it so the map faces you."

You flip the map around and stare at it. "I don't see anything."

"Watch this," he says, and moves towards you. Suddenly, the growths on Feared Beard's face start pushing through the holes in the map—holes that are right on the island he had pointed out. They weren't from wear and tear—Feared Beard put those holes there on purpose.

You look closer. There's a tiny X marked on the island.

"That's me real treasure," Feared Beard says. "Those other Xs are worthless. But beware," he continues. "See the path to the treasure?"

You nod.

"Don't go that way. Booby traps galore. Follow me beard to the true path."

"That is totally gross," you say, but you take a good look at the map. One of Feared Beard's facial worms points to a patch of land labelled *Death's Swamp*.

"You want me to go through there?"

"It's not such a bad place," Feared Beard says. "As long as you don't mind the snakes."

"I *do* mind the snakes," you say. You're about to say more when Feared Beard suddenly disappears into the fog.

Then a big hand clamps down on your shoulder, while another snatches the map away from you.

"Caught you red-handed!" a booming voice snarls.

Startled, you whip around to see Captain John's men have surrounded you.

"Looks like you're coming with us," the one holding you says.

Turn to page 10.

The first door opens as you approach. You swim through and—

"Gaaah!"

Floating in the water before you is the scuba team. They're not moving and their tanks are still strapped to their backs, but no air bubbles are coming up. As you move towards one of them, you realize why—they've all been turned to stone.

You turn around. You've got to get out of here, back to the surface, back to safety.

But instead of the doorway, you're facing the merman statue. It's followed you in here. It looms close, and all you can see is its rigid stone face. The statue's eyes glow red. You reach out to shield your face, but your hands begin to feel like they're encased in cement. You stare at them. They're cold. Heavy. And turning grey.

"No!" you think, feeling the cold grip of the transformation. A burst of bubbles escapes your lips.

And then the bubbles are no more.

THE END.

To try again, go back to page 106.

You push through the second door and freak out as you're thrust into a dark chamber.

Oh no! you think. *I've chosen certain doom. Dang!*

The chamber fills with pinpricks of eerie red light. Certain doom for sure! This place must be filled with more statues. All with glowing red eyes, right? Only . . .

You narrow your gaze, moving towards the pairs of glittering red eyes. That's right, *glittering.*

You gasp, but not with fear this time. You realize what you're staring at. Rubies. They're lining the entire room.

You flick your light on and are amazed at the vast treasure. Golden objects, obviously belonging to whoever this statue's people were, fill your field of vision.

"Nobody ever chooses the second door," the statue says. "You are nearly the first . . ."

Nearly?

"Only one other has found this treasure. He took what he could carry. And once more, you must take only what you can carry. You may visit this chamber only once . . ."

Then the coral hull of the ship is pulled open. You look down at the jewels and scoop up as many as you can.

But the opening is not long-lived. After a few moments it starts to shut again.

You ignore the coins spilling from your hands and race through the opening before the hull closes around it.

You're rich! Rich beyond your wildest dreams! You kick your flippers and make your way to the surface.

As you get closer, you hear a whirring through the water. A dark shape passes overhead.

It's strange that a boat would be here just as you've managed to grab some of the treasure. You push yourself a bit further, hopefully out of range of the boat, and carefully pop your head up.

You make out two figures on board. It's hard to see clearly through your mask, but then you recognize their voices, their movements—"Mom! Dad!"

They whirl around to face you. You swim towards them, careful not to lose the jewels in your excitement.

Once you're at the boat, they pull you aboard. The glittering treasure from below spills out of your suit.

Your memory is still foggy, but your dad claps you on the back, smiling brightly. "We knew you could do it."

You shake your head, not understanding.

"Your memory will return soon," your mom says.

Maybe so, but for now it doesn't matter. You've found your parents—and the treasure of a lifetime.

00:00
You survived! There are eleven other ways to escape the danger— try to find them all!

no way you're telling this ghost anything. You look around. The shore is within running distance, and the fog is now thick enough to give you ample cover.

"Go haunt those other guys," you tell Feared Beard, then make a break for the shore.

As you run, Feared Beard materializes in the fog. "I wouldn't do that if I were ye . . ."

Once again you give a startled scream, only this time it's because you've managed to trip over one of the rocks. Blood seeps from a wound on your ankle.

"Will you stop that!" you shout.

And then, from somewhere in the soupy fog, you hear real people talking to one another. They know you're out here.

"Now look what you did," you hiss at the ghost.

"I apologize," Feared Beard says. "But I really wouldn't go out in the water if I were you. Not in the condition you're in." He points to your leg.

But you don't have time to argue. The men are getting closer and you need to make a move.

If you take Feared Beard's advice, turn to page 58.
If you swim away, turn to page 138.

The speedboat is fast and it's heading your way. Besides, you'll make it way farther *on* the water than in it.

So you wave your hands frantically, even though it means you're flailing helplessly in the ocean. Gulping back sea water, you scream at the top of your lungs. But you can't be heard over the roaring engine as the boat comes closer, and closer.

You close your eyes as the boat speeds over to you, and then—

You're hit in the face with a wall of sea spray.

Choking on sea water again, you look up at the driver silhouetted against the clouds. She kicks a rope ladder off the edge of the boat. "Come on. Quick," she says, and you don't hesitate to grab it.

You spill over the gunwale and onto the deck, shivering and coughing. When you've caught your breath, you lean back against the side of the boat and take a moment to regard your rescuer.

She's young—barely older than you—and dressed all in black. Plus, despite having driven a boat at top speed, she doesn't look the least bit windswept. Clearly she knows her way around the ocean.

"It was lucky that I found you, especially before anyone, or any*thing*, else did." Then she extends her hand. "I'm Erin, by the way."

You shake her hand, trying to piece together what exactly she meant by that.

"Now that you're not about to drown or get flattened by my boat, why don't you tell me what's brought you to the open Atlantic? I've been . . . working . . . in this area for a while now, and it's pretty much all tour boats and lobster traps." She pauses, then smirks. "You look like you have a story to tell."

There's definitely something going on with this woman. You're sure she knows more than she's letting on, and you have a sinking feeling she's somehow part of this whole thing. Your first instinct is to keep the map hidden and say the bare minimum about your predicament. The less she knows, the better. But maybe there's another option. If you show her the map, she might help you get where you need to go. It's worth a shot, isn't it?

If you keep the map hidden, turn to page 8.
If you show Erin the map, turn to page 96.

"Cowabunga!" you holler at the top of your lungs.

Erin whirls around, a look of shock on her face. You run towards her at top speed. You can't possibly miss at this range. You're going to tackle her, grab the map, and get the upper hand.

"No!" she blurts. "You don't understand . . ."

You smile as you race forward. You don't even worry about slowing down. You're already jumping through the air. You reach out towards Erin but she sidesteps you, and that's when you see it . . .

Erin hadn't been looking at the ground by her feet.

She'd been looking at the ground below where she was standing.

At the edge of a cliff.

And now you're in free fall, going down—and fast.

As you open your mouth to scream, you notice something rushing towards you.

Hey, it's an X on the ground. Like the one from the map. It fills your entire field of vision, getting bigger, and bigger, and—

THE END.
To try again, go back to page 21.

"**E**rin," you say, hoping you'll scare the map right out of her hands. You almost do.

Erin jumps at your voice. She whirls around, and you can read a lot from the look of disbelief on her face. *"You?"* she says. "I thought you were . . ."

"Dead?" you finish.

Erin backs away from you. It's only a few steps, but the fog is beginning to swallow her up. Maybe you seemed like a helpless kid a few minutes ago, but now you've shown Erin you've got more grit than she thought.

"About that," she says.

"Don't start," you say. "There's only one way off this island. And that's working together." She doesn't say anything for a moment, so you add, "You know about this area, but this is my dad's map. I can find that treasure."

She narrows her eyes. "Fine. If we find it, you'll get your cut," she says.

"Great," you reply, although you don't honestly believe she'll split the treasure with you. But you'll worry about those details later. She hasn't killed you yet, so maybe your luck will hold out.

You reach a hand out to her. "Give me the map, Erin, and let's find that treasure."

She doesn't quite let go of it, so you have to pluck it from her fingers. Erin stands right above you as you pore over the map's details.

As you try to work out the path to take, Erin fishes something out of her jacket. You look over and smile when you see what she has.

A compass. Mom and Dad made sure you knew how to use one. No matter how foggy the island is, it will point north. And now all you have to do is follow the needle, because that X on the map is right at the northern tip of the island.

The needle spins and wobbles but eventually settles on one direction. "North," Erin says.

In the back of your mind, something pings. This compass is acting weird. You've never seen a needle spin around like that. You could trust your instinct and try to get back to the boat. But is it really worth questioning when you're so close to the treasure?

If you follow the compass, turn to page 35.

If you go back to the boat, turn to page 37.

Down, down you go.

You try to flick your headlights back on, but they're not working. All you see is the rock wall rushing past as you descend deeper and deeper.

You eye the depth gauge. Four hundred metres down! How are you ever going to get back to the surface, especially with no power and a limited supply of air?

You begin to shake. Is it the pressure affecting you? Or just fear pumping through your body?

You look outside again, catching glimpses of other bioluminescent creatures bobbing in the ocean current. Freakish-looking anglerfish with huge eyes and jaws rush past you. The water is pitch black. This is the end, you realize. There's no escaping your undersea prison.

You try to breathe calmly, steadily as you accept your fate.

Only . . .

Something is creating light. Another one of those creatures? Do you have it in you to fight?

But this light is more intense than a lone creature can produce. It nearly blinds you as it fills the submersible. You try to see what could be causing it. In doing so, you push against one of the controls, causing the sub to spin in the water, and you catch sight of—

"No! It can't be!"

But it is. The abyss opens up to reveal a huge cavern. Below you, a massive undersea city stretches out in all directions. You spy buildings and movement beyond the dome that surrounds the entire place. There are even creatures down there. Creatures with arms and legs.

A word bubbles into your consciousness.

"Atlantis," you breathe.

Without power, you have no way of piloting the submersible as it moves closer to the dome.

And then—*SPLOOSH!*—you pass right through the cloud-like layer of membranous goo that holds the city in place. You stare at the cityscape, now much clearer, as the sub touches down.

You've arrived.

Turn to page 102.

"**S**orry, Erin, but I was raised better than that," you say, as you take a deep breath and dive off the boat.

The water is frigid, and the current pushes you back towards the boat, but a surge of adrenalin gives you the energy to swim forward.

As you get closer to the pilot, the smoke pouring out of the damaged plane fills your lungs and you start to cough. Then a moment later, you feel slick engine oil begin to coat your skin and clothing. If the plane explodes or a bigger fire breaks out, you're in trouble.

The pilot, who is bleeding from the head, sees you approaching. "Knife!" he blurts, and points to the rock, which is now right in front of you.

You nod, pick it up, and toss it to him. He quickly cuts the remaining lines.

As he drops into the water beside you, you hear a small explosion. You look towards the plane and see the engine has caught fire. A wave of heat pushes towards you, singeing your skin and sucking your breath away.

Only moments to go before you're roasted . . .

You've got to get away from the flaming plane and

the patch of fiery oil. Your lungs gasp for air, and you wonder about the pilot, who looks faint and dizzy.

You grab hold of his arm and swim as hard as you can towards the boat. At least this time the current is on your side! Plus, the explosion seems to have pushed the fog out, at least temporarily.

Just then, the entire plane explodes into a ball of fire and debris that engulfs the spot the pilot had been hanging in moments earlier. You watch in shock, silently cursing Erin and her "probably safe" assessment.

"Thanks," the pilot gasps.

"Don't thank me yet," you say. "And besides, you were trying to kill me!"

"Not anymore," he says. "I was just under orders. Didn't realize it was a kid I was trying to bump off."

The pilot reaches a hand out to you. "Seriously. You saved my life. I owe you at least the same. You help me find that treasure, and I'll make sure you get out of here safely."

You consider this for a moment. This pilot, whoever he is, might be a more trustworthy partner than Erin, especially if he thinks he owes you. Speaking of Erin, you don't see her on the boat deck. Where is she?

A minute later, you spot her by the sea caves. She's soaking wet and huddled over a wooden box.

She found the treasure without you!

And she's so close to her boat. It would be nothing

for her to take the treasure and leave you there. If you make a deal with the pilot, maybe he can help stop Erin from double-crossing you.

Then again, maybe you've made enough deals for today.

If you take the pilot's deal, turn to page 3.

If you swim out to Erin by yourself, turn to page 5.

Erin's right. The pilot will be fine on his own. You turn your attention to the shimmering object below the surface of the water. There must be more where that came from, right?

"Spot me for a minute," you say to Erin. "I think I might have a lead on that treasure." You point out the object to Erin, then gird yourself for a jump into the Atlantic. You gulp a deep breath of air, close your eyes, and plunge. Those swimming lessons sure come in handy as you swim down through the strong current. You try to keep your focus on the gold object while also scanning the ocean floor. There! It's just a few metres away—an actual treasure chest!

And that shimmering thing you saw from the boat? A gold coin. Some of them have spilled out of the chest, which has no lock that you can see. What else is in that box? Jewels? The fortune of a lifetime? More?

You almost gasp, but you're smart enough to hold on to the air in your lungs.

As you swim towards the chest, the current pulls at you, and you have to flail your legs and arms to stay near the treasure. You're burning energy—and oxygen. You feel a tightness in your lungs.

How long have you been holding your air? Thirty seconds? A minute?

You hear splashing above you. You crane your neck to see Erin and the pilot—who clearly *was* okay on his own—struggling in the water. You're almost out of air, but you're so close to the chest. You could push for a few more seconds and try to get it open, or you could grab as many gold coins as you can for now and go back later for the rest.

If you open the chest, turn to page 12.

If you grab all the coins you can, turn to page 60.

If you open the chest, turn to page 12.
If you grab all the coins you can, turn to page 60.

02:59

aptain John and his crew are the least of your worries now. You race down the steps, tripping once or twice but quickly regaining your footing. Then you have a better idea. You hop onto the railing and slide down like you're on the jungle gym at school.

"WHOOPEE!" you scream, almost enjoying the feeling of spinning around and around. You reach the bottom quickly, jump off the railing, and sprint towards the door.

"RAAAAARRRGGGHHH!" the monster bellows. No! It's positioned right outside the open door. As you turn on your heel and head back to the stairs, you start to scream.

But your scream is cut short as one of its python-like tentacles shoots into the room, grabbing hold of your waist. You try to pry yourself loose, but the creature's plate-sized suckers keep you from slipping free.

Then you're lowered towards its open mouth. You look deep into its massive maw, smell its rotten, fishy breath, and—

THE END.

To try again, go back to page 54.
To try again, go back to page 54.

The boat is down below, but so is that monster. And a bunch of men trying to grab you. Racing to the top of the lighthouse should buy you time, so that's what you do.

Exasperated and out of breath, you finally make it. The view from here is incredible. For a moment you are overcome with the feeling of serenity that some of those old lightkeepers must have felt—

"RAAAAARRRGGGHHH!"

The sea creature is pounding its gigantic tentacles against the side of the lighthouse. Its massive suckers stick to the walls, and when the creature pulls its tentacles back, chunks of rock and concrete rain down.

The ground at your feet shakes. *This thing's going to send the entire lighthouse crashing down!*

Then you remember—the flare gun!

You've been so preoccupied you haven't thought to use it. You grip it tightly and aim it right at the creature. "Suck on THIS!" you yell, and squeeze the trigger.

There's a massive bang and a huge flash of light as the flare shoots right at the creature—

Turn to page 100.

"**D**eath's Swamp," you say, under your breath.

"What was that?" one of the men asks.

"Uh, nothing."

Then you step off the path and into the swamp.

"Hey, kid. What are you doing?"

You look down at your feet, now ankle deep in putrid, swampy water. "Uh . . . rinsing off my shoes?"

"Get out of there," he says.

But instead you take another step.

"Come on, we don't have all day."

You wade farther into the swamp. Now you're up to your knees. Mosquitoes buzz around you. You slap at them as they start to bite.

During all of this you notice these guys don't take a single step after you. And that's exactly what you were hoping for.

The man with the map has ignored you completely. He's eyeing the stone footpath.

"Forget about the kid," he says. "The treasure's this way."

The men make their way down the path, with the last one turning to jab a threatening finger your way. "We'll be back for you," he says.

"Sure thing," you return, playing in the swamp like you're at the local outdoor pool.

You keep up the ruse until they're out of view.

Then you let out a shaky breath and start moving across the swamp. This is beyond gross. You're going to need at least five showers and a power spray to hose off all this muck—

You hear shouts up ahead.

And then a heavy thump.

"Feared Beard was right," you say, staring in the direction of the path.

There *were* booby traps after all.

You wonder if you should check to see whether those crooks are okay, but you worry there could be more booby traps along the path. Instead you look across the swamp and sigh. It takes longer than you'd like to trudge to the other side, and yes, there are snakes. Lots of them. You keep feeling them slither past you. Thankfully, none of them bite. But you're completely coated in the swamp's stinky film by the time you pull yourself back onto dry land. You're so grossed out you don't even notice it at first, until you're practically standing over it—

There is an X marked with rocks on the ground.

And a shovel lying right beside it.

You don't need to be told what to do. Picking up the shovel, you dig through the compacted earth until the blade bangs against something hard.

A treasure chest.

Carefully, you expose the lid. Using the end of the shovel, you pry it open, and—

"GAAAH!" you scream. Because, sure enough, Feared Beard's skeletal left hand is inside the chest. The fingers are curled so the thumb is sticking up your way, like he's giving you a disembodied thumbs-up from beyond the grave.

"Gross me out!" you blurt.

You move the hand aside with your shovel, only to reveal that the chest is full of glittering jewels and gold coins. You've hit pay dirt!

You drop to your knees to start filling your pockets with as much as you can carry, then remember—weren't you supposed to bring that hand back to Feared Beard?

If you keep your promise to Feared Beard, turn to page 15.

If you leave the hand and take only the treasure, turn to page 13.

The man holding the map takes a look at it. "Death's Swamp," he says, quizzically. He makes a face. So do the others. So do you, in fact. It's primarily from the stench of the place, like hundreds of dead things are rotting below the surface!

"I say we take the path," the man says. You're inclined to agree.

You all plug your noses as you stay to the path. At least you're not wading ankle—or hip—deep in those putrid waters. Soon you wind away from the swamp and through more rocky outcrops. You're descending now, and the rock walls on either side of you are getting closer and closer together.

The leader follows the map closely. "This must be it," he says, running his finger along a dotted line that ends at the X. "Feared Beard's treasure should be just around the bend."

You wrinkle your brow. "This is pretty easy," you say.

"Too easy," you hear from one of the men behind you. "I thought there were supposed to be booby traps."

You take a few steps forward but trip over a thick root twisting out of the path.

"Oof!" you manage, as you're thrown to the rocky

ground, the wind momentarily knocked from your lungs.

As you lie there trying to heave the air back into you, you notice one of the rocks you've fallen on is slowly sinking into the muddy earth. Sure, rocks can move under your weight, but not this much. And it's not just that rock that's sinking, it's several of them.

You turn around to see that the knobby root you tripped over isn't any ordinary root. It's some kind of antiquated lever. You follow its path as it winds up the rock wall. You hear a click, then see large shadows rolling over the edge of the cliff above you.

You get up and try to run but—

CRASH!

A large boulder smashes to the ground just ahead of you, blocking your escape. You turn, only to find that—

SMASH!

Another boulder has blocked the path behind you.

The four of you look up as more boulders roll into view.

Right. Above. You.

CRUNCH!

THE END.

To try again, go back to page 136.

kay, so they're big, but they're still only lobsters. They might be your size, and armed with pincers and crushers, but you've got . . .

Just rocks.

"And my wits," you tell yourself. "I can do this!"

You pick up the nearest rock and hurl it. "Ha! Take that!" you shout, and watch as it bounces off the lobster's thick exoskeleton. The lobster's massive eye droops down to regard the non-damage you've caused it. Then it snaps its pincer at you.

You scramble to your feet and take a couple of steps back, then look over your shoulder to find a sizeable cliff. Not to worry, though. You'd just fall onto the sharp-looking rocks being lashed by the ocean.

You take another tiny step back and nearly slip on the slick rocks. That would have been close—

Wait! That's the ticket to defeating these things. Get them to wipe out on the rocks and take a lethal tumble. The two lobsters come barrelling at you. You've only got one shot. As the gargantuan crustaceans race towards you, you dodge.

If you dodge left, turn to page 117.

If you dodge right, turn to page 118.

Fighting mutant lobsters is not what you signed up for today. You turn and run. Only it's not such an impressive run. The slippery rocks mean you're constantly tripping and falling and scraping yourself.

Even worse—those lobsters are following you. And they're much better at this than you are.

You'll need to get to the fishing village—even if it is abandoned—and then maybe back to the mainland. Are those lobsters going to outrun you the whole way? Or do you have what it takes to outrun some lob—

"EAAAAAUGH!" you scream.

Because you're falling.

Darkness blankets you on all sides.

And then, *WHUMP*.

It takes you a few moments to realize what's happened. You've slipped down a crack in the rocks. But it's more than just a crack. You're some distance below the surface now. The only light seems to be coming from that crack way above you.

As your eyes gradually adjust to the darkness, you can see that climbing back out will be almost impossible. The walls of the cavern you're trapped in are too steep, and the exit too high.

"Drats," you say, kind of impressed that you've gone this far through life without having used the word "drats" . . . until now.

Maybe there's another way out of here. You turn, straining to see through the darkness. You must be close to the ocean; maybe you can swim out.

But there's very little sea water penetrating this cavern.

You take a few steps forward and your feet clunk against something heavy. At first, you mistake it for a rock. There are rocks all over the place. But it isn't a rock.

It's a treasure chest!

Wait, no—even better—IT'S TWO TREASURE CHESTS! They're just sitting there, side by side, closed lids and all. What the—?

It's almost like the chests want you to choose which one to open. And who are you to say no to that?

If you choose the chest on the left, turn to page 125.
If you choose the chest on the right, turn to page 127.

It's a good thing you showed up when you did or that treasure might have been lost forever! You swim over and try to grab hold of the chest, but the thing is too darn heavy and keeps slipping out of your hands.

Then you remember you're wearing scuba gear and there are all kinds of gadgets hooked to you. You look down, and . . . *A-ha!* You've got some extra clips dangling from your weight belt. And there's a latch on the lid of the chest.

You swim closer. Sure enough, when you sit down beside the chest, the clip reaches just far enough to click into place.

Great! You can totally do this, especially now that your hands and legs are free to kick and push through the water. You start to propel yourself backwards, away from the chasm, but as you do you feel another strong current against your back, and—

Oh no—you're toppling over!

You reach down to unclip the chest, but it tips over the edge of the chasm and drops like a stone, spilling its jewels and gold coins and taking you with it . . . down, down, down . . .

You try again to unclip yourself, but the weight of

the chest is pulling against the clip—and your weight belt. There's no way to unfasten yourself.

As you're pulled down, you notice the traces of sunlight from above are slipping away. The water gets colder and colder.

Your panicked breathing registers on the oxygen gauge—the deeper you go, the greater the pressure, and you're using up what's left in your tank really quickly. Your ears pound as the pressure builds.

Deeper, deeper you go.

THE END.
To try again, go back to page 106.

As you enter the wreck, much of the light is extinguished. Only small gaps in the hull allow light to trickle into the ship.

But what those small beams reveal astounds you. The entire ship is composed of that strange substance. You run your hand along it and quickly pull away. It *is* coral. It's sharp, and a small cloud of your own blood floats in the water before dissipating.

A boat made from living material?

You turn on your light and train it around the room you're in.

A human face—pale and ominous—greets you.

You scream, dropping your regulator.

Then, fighting to fit your only source of air back into your mouth, you once again shine your light on the face.

It's a man with a heavy beard—but he's solid stone.

A statue.

Breathing with some relief, you take in the details around you. The statue stands in the chamber you're in, right in front of two doors. But the statue is only half-man. Its lower portion is a fish's tail. A merman? Huh?

Your light also illuminates flashes of gold, and your

eyes move past the statue to the coins that litter the floor.

That statue is probably worth a fortune. The boat must be too. But for now the only things you'll be able to bring up to the surface are those gold coins. And you still don't know where the divers are.

You reach down to grab a fistful of coins, but as you right yourself the room fills with an eerie red glow.

Then you see it.

The statue's eyes are blood red.

You scream again, this time dropping the coins. You swim back to the edge of the room, but something's not right.

You turn. There *was* an opening here before, wasn't there? You're sure this is where you came from. Has the coral grown over the hole already?

You turn back around, looking for any way out, but all that's in the room is the statue with its glowing eyes and the two doors behind it.

Then the statue glides your way.

Impossible!

You sway in the water, helpless, as it moves closer and opens its mouth. Sound travels differently in water, but you can hear its voice clearly, almost like it's projecting thoughts into your head.

"You have disturbed my slumber!" it says coldly.

You try to talk, to apologize, but you can't with

the regulator in your mouth. Still, you hear your own thoughts in your head. You let them out, slowly.

I . . . I didn't mean to . . . I was just looking for my parents . . .

"You have but two exits. A door will open when you approach."

. . . Approach . . . ?

"You seek the treasure. The two-legs all do."

. . . Fair enough . . .

"You shall have it. But you shall choose."

Choose?

"One door leads to treasure; the other to doom."

You shake your head. *What if I turn back?*

"There is no turning back," the statue tells you. "There is only forward."

You realize this thing is right. It might control your path, but the first choice is yours.

If you choose the first door, turn to page 65.
If you choose the second door, turn to page 66.

There's only one thing you know for sure, and it's that you need to follow the map. You might not be able to trust Erin, but she seems to know her way around these waters. And she has a boat. Those are two big pluses.

You decide to show her the map and give her the short version of what happened earlier. Which isn't hard, considering how little you still remember. As you suspected, she doesn't seem to care so much about the details. The map, though, is a different story.

"I knew it," she whispers. "I knew I'd find it eventually. Listen, kid. This can be a win-win situation. We'll split whatever we find, and you'll still have more than enough to save your folks. But if anyone asks, you never saw me. Deal?"

You're not sure *what* her "deal" is, but you think about it for a moment, then agree. You shake on it before you both turn your attention back to the map.

You point out that there are multiple Xs marked on it. "Which one should we follow?" you ask.

Erin furrows her brow, thinking. "One is marking a point over water. We'll need scuba gear to explore there, and that should be our last attempt. But this island," she says, pointing to a piece of land at the edge of the map, "is the closest point."

You nod, making a mental note of the map and where exactly the X is on the island. Then Erin motions to the empty seat beside her.

"You might want to hold on to something," she says with a wink, and then she hits the throttle. Hard. You lurch back into your seat as the engine roars and the boat cuts through the water.

You debate if you've made the right decision. Erin didn't seem to care one way or the other about you or your parents. She just keeps looking from the map to the open sea, a big grin across her face.

And, you wonder, is she planning to sabotage your deal and make it a double win for herself? It's not like she radioed for help when she spotted you in the ocean.

In fact, looking around, you realize this boat doesn't even seem to *have* a radio. You might have just made a huge mistake.

Up ahead, a dark shape emerges in the distance. The island!

You're coming up on it fast now. Does Erin know this boat can do anything other than top speed? Then, just ahead of the island, something else drifts into view.

Erin slows the boat down, barely, a quizzical look on her face.

"What is it?" you say, still not understanding.

"Fog bank," she says. "But it's moving in too fast."

"Maybe we'd better call the coast guard," you say, hoping she'll take the bait.

Erin looks at you and frowns. "I've dealt with worse," she snaps.

Erin pushes ahead, following the map, and a minute later you're swallowed by the thick fog. You've been to the Maritimes before, but Erin was right: this fog feels different.

Not only has it completely enveloped the boat, but it's absorbed the sound of the ocean around you. The air is still and the water silent. Ahead, you barely make out the skeletal edge of the island. It's almost like the bank of fog inhabits this place.

Erin shakes her head, then reverses the boat. "There's got to be a better way to get to the island," she says, and as she steers back out of the fog, you emerge into waters that are recognizably ocean.

But now there's a new problem. A seaplane is overhead. Normally this wouldn't concern you, but it's headed your way and flying lower and lower. It's definitely following the boat.

Is someone on your tail? Or are they on *Erin's*?

Either way, someone else knows about this island. And you need to make sure they don't get to the treasure before you do. But how?

You could stick with Erin and hope she holds up her end of the bargain. Or you can ditch her, and this boat, and try to make it on your own.

If you grab the map and jump into the water, turn to page 21.

If you stay on the boat and take your chances with Erin, turn to page 22.

01:34

nd bounces harmlessly off its thick skin.
"Aw, nuts!"

If anything, you've only made it angrier. It doubles its speed, pulling its bulky body up the side of the lighthouse and coating everything with a dripping, foul slime.

You wrinkle your nose in disgust and brace yourself as the lighthouse begins to sway. *This thing is going to topple!* There's only one way to get out of here, you realize . . .

You hold your ground, waiting for the right moment.

Then the tower pitches in one direction. *It's now or never!*

So you run.

And jump.

For a second you're flying in mid-air, but then you see it coming—fast.

THE TENTACLE!

You grab it with both hands. The slime makes you nearly lose your grip, but you keep holding tight. The entire lighthouse is coming down now—along with the creature itself!

The ground rushes up to meet you.

Letting go of the tentacle, you try to drop and roll and end up splayed out along the rocks. You leap to your feet and run as fast as you can—

SMASH!

You jump as the lighthouse crashes into the rocks.

What's left of it lies there like a discarded log. And underneath the lighthouse, squashed like a bug, is the creature.

"Urgh," you say, once you catch a whiff of it.

Slowly you manage to get back onto your feet. You're wobbling unsteadily, mostly from the shock of it all.

You look around, realizing the boat is gone and the men who were chasing you are nowhere to be seen. In the distance you can hear the coast guard's sirens. It won't be long until they get here.

And, hey, you remember as you reach inside your shirt. You've still got that treasure map!

00:00

You survived! There are eleven other ways to escape the danger— try to find them all!

You open the submersible's hatch and plop down onto a strangely moving seabed. That weird membrane covers the bottom of the city as well. It seems to support your weight well enough, but it wobbles under your steps.

When you look up, you are amazed to see a cluster of tall, muscular people standing in front of you. Most of them are wearing clothes made from sea animals: fish scales, sharkskin and even a few spiky caps that look like they came from sea urchins.

"Another from the surface has come to join us," one of them says.

"Join you?" you say. Then you wonder—how do these guys know English?

"Welcome to Atlantis," the closest one says. He is a young man with a head of flowing brown hair. He looks like the kind of super-buff dude who would be advertising a gym on TV.

He reaches out, and you shake his hand. He seems confused by this, and you realize that maybe down here in the city of Atlantis, they fist bump instead. You try to fist bump this guy, only . . . nope. He seems confused by that too.

"Follow me," he says, and leads you to one of the closest buildings. It is a long, domed structure that seems grown from coral rather than built.

The building material, whatever it is, parts into a doorway. You follow the man inside and are taken through a grand hall. A long table set with golden plates and cutlery and piled with all manner of seafood stretches out endlessly. The Atlanteans sitting at the table look up at you.

"Others have descended from the surface," the man says.

"Oh, great!" you say. "That means you can get me back up there . . ."

"Impossible," the man returns. "The city of Atlantis is lost to the rest of the world. If they were to find us, they would destroy all that we have. You must stay. Please, join us for a meal."

If you sit down to dinner, turn to page 31.
If you get the heck out of there, turn to page 33.

You watch as Erin races off into the distance. Once you're sure she can no longer see you, you pull the map out of your shirt and take a close look at it for the first time. As you study it, you discover some of the places and landmarks match this area of the Atlantic. There are a few Xs on it: one over the water, one on an island and one on a small peninsula.

If you're right—and with a dad who made certain you could read a map correctly, you're pretty sure you are—that peninsula is the one you're standing on right now.

Yes, this is where you need to be. That treasure must be around here somewhere. And, you hope, your parents!

You need to get the lay of the land first. You clamber over rocks and boulders until you reach high ground, which looks over the entire peninsula. It's dotted with ramshackle fishing huts that look like they've been warped and battered from years of exposure to sea and weather.

You pull out the map again and check your surroundings. Yes, this is definitely the place. The X is near the end of the peninsula, close to the water but on the side opposite where you arrived.

You make your way back down the rocky path towards your target. There are large outcrops of boulders, and some thick patches of forest that make it difficult to see to the water's edge. A cool wind blows from across the ocean, and you shiver in your still-wet clothes. Even though this place seems abandoned, you feel like you're not alone.

CLUNK, CLUNK, CLUNK.

You jump. As you scan your surroundings, you see the shutters of one of the fishing shacks knocking against the siding.

Then, narrowing your eyes, you notice something else. There's movement inside the cabin. You shake your head. It's probably just the wind blowing through the drafty hut.

Out of the corner of your eye, you catch another trail of movement beyond the huts, this time down by the rocks leading towards the edge of the peninsula. If you're going to find the treasure, you need to know what you're dealing with. But where do you start?

If you check out the hut, turn to page 49.

If you explore the rocky area along the shore, turn to page 52.

Y ou don't know anything about speedboats or light-houses, but you've been diving a couple of times. That must be a good sign, right? Dive boat it is!

You paddle madly through the water towards the boat, which bobs up and down on the waves. You can't see anyone on deck, but maybe they're out of view. "Help!" you shout once, twice. You try waving your arms to attract attention. Still no response.

You notice oxygen tanks tied to one side of the boat. On the other side is something cylindrical but much larger.

A red flag on a small buoy floating just beside the boat catches your eye. You know it means "diver down." There must be people somewhere below the surface.

The current pushes you closer to the boat, and you swim over to the stern, pull yourself up the ladder, and spill onto the deck. You lie there for a moment, breathing heavily and shivering in the cold air.

You tilt your head to take in the larger object secured to the side of the boat. It's some kind of one-person submersible.

When you've managed to get past the wave of fatigue, you haul yourself to your feet and stagger towards the bow of the boat. It's completely deserted, you realize.

You shake your head. This can't be right. Shouldn't there be somebody up here in case of an emergency? The question keeps pounding away at you: Where *is* everybody?

The wind whips against your wet clothes, raising goosebumps and making you shiver.

As you hug your arms to your body, you feel the map under your shirt and pull it out. Staring down at it, you notice it includes a coastline—this coastline, by the looks of it—and that there are a few points marked with Xs. One X is located along the coast, another on a nearby island and one over water.

Maybe close to where this dive boat is anchored?

You're not going to find any more answers on the deck of the boat, and you're not about to drive off with it while there are divers down there. Looks like you're going below the surface. You could suit up for a dive. Or you could try taking that submersible for a spin . . .

If you scuba dive, turn to page 46.
If you take the submersible, turn to page 47.

You figure you should at least hear what the scientist has to say first. You can always grab a bowl of chowder later. You climb back down the ladder and face the woman.

"You've done very well," the scientist says. "Please, follow me."

She opens a door, and you step into a comfy-looking room. Inside, there's a roaring fireplace, walls lined with bookshelves and two armchairs by the fire. Sitting in them are—

Impossible! What are they doing here?

"Mom! Dad!"

"Don't worry," your dad says, standing up to greet you. "Everything will be clear in just a moment."

Then your mom looks past you to the doorway. "Excellent. You've arrived just in time."

You whirl around to see Erin standing there.

"Gaaaaak!" you exclaim. "What is *she* doing here?"

"Do you still have it?" your mom asks you.

You shake your head. "What? My sanity? Not anymore."

"The map," your dad says. "You still have it, correct?"

You instinctively pat your shirt. The map is still

there, safely concealed. You reach under your shirt to pull it out.

"Please tell me there's a reasonable explanation for all of this," you whimper.

Your parents come towards you. Your mom gives you a much-needed hug, while your dad takes the map from you.

"Of course. We just needed to make sure you were ready," he begins.

"Ready for what?" Somebody has turned the world upside down and set it to brain-scrambling mode.

"To join the family business, of course. Our family has been treasure hunters, among other things, for generations now."

"Our family?"

"You probably don't remember your cousin Erin."

You do a double take. "Huh?"

"It was her idea to temporarily erase your memory. To see if you were ready to take up the challenge. And to join us in our professional endeavours."

Your mind is swimming. But then you look past your parents to the books on the shelves. They're all about crime, burglary and the law, and you know for a fact you're not from a family of lawyers.

And, pinned to the wall beside one bookshelf are old newspaper and magazine clippings. The words "HEIST" and "MILLIONS STOLEN" and "WHO ARE

THE ENIGMA CLAN?" jump out at you. You sound out those last words. "Enigma Clan?"

Your mom shrugs. "We didn't make that name up, but it's stuck."

You shake your head, moving away from Erin, your parents . . . This can't be true. It can't be happening . . . You're part of a family of master criminals?

Your father reaches into his pocket and pulls out a vial with a green fluid inside. "Your memory will come back when you take this," he says, with a grin. "Drink up; we've got a treasure to find."

He hands you the vial. You stare at it quizzically. What other choice do you have? You bring it to your lips, take a sip, and . . .

00:00

You survived! There are eleven other ways to escape the danger—try to find them all!

Before that scientist has a chance to explain, you form your palms into a makeshift cup, scoop out a handful of watery chowder, and take a sip.

"Mmm. Chowder!" you say.

"It's not chowder!" the scientist returns. Then, a second later. "You didn't . . . You didn't *drink* it, did you?"

The overpowering smell and taste compel you to take another sip.

"You *did* drink it!" the scientist says. Her jaw hangs slack. She staggers backwards, shaking her head. "No person has ever drunk it before."

You blink at her. "What do you mean . . . no *person*?"

Your stomach gurgles. Man, you're super hungry. You step down from the ladder and approach the scientist, who backs away from you.

"We've been using it on the animals," she says, her voice a whisper. "We got the formula from a group in the Rocky Mountains. It's how they change, you see."

"Change . . . ?"

Your stomach gurgles again, but not from hunger. You open your mouth to give a big belch. As you put a hand to your face, you realize that instead of teeth, you have strange moving mouthparts.

And your hands. They're not hands. Your fingers are fusing together. Forming claws. Big red claws! And your skin—it's no longer skin. It's being coated with a hard shell-like substance.

You let out a scream—or at least try to with that strange new mouth of yours—and drop to the ground. Your legs are becoming thinner. Six more of them pop out of your sides.

You look up at the scientist, trying to plead for help, but she's already whipped out her phone to record whatever it is you're transforming into.

You scuttle about on the floor, looking for a means of escape. But all you end up doing is bumping into an aquarium. You give a terrified grunt at the creature you see inside: half-human, half-lobster. Then you realize that the tank is empty.

You're staring at your own reflection!

THE END.

To try again, go back to page 104.

You didn't come this far to walk away from the treasure, or your parents. You reach the submersible's clawed arms towards the rusted padlock securing the chest. You quickly snap it open and pull it away.

You gingerly hook one claw over the loop of metal that remains fixed to the chest, then lift the lid.

It doesn't open easily, though. Either the lid is too heavy or whatever is inside has been under so much pressure that a vacuum seal has formed.

You pull back against the lid. You can hear the sub's gears grinding, trying to work against the heavy forces. For a second, you wonder if you're going to break the submersible's claw, but then the wooden lid pops right off the chest, landing on the edge of the chasm.

You press your face against the curved window, trying to get a better view in the dim waters. But there's no gleam of gold inside the chest—just a dark, gaping void.

That's when you begin to notice sand from the surrounding sea floor is being pulled up and into the chest.

More and more sand is whipping around, along with small fishes and bits of coral and sea debris. Now some kind of waterspout is forming around the base of the chest. How can this be?

You pull back on the controls to move the submersible away from the strange chest, but now *you're* being drawn towards it as well. There's no way you can fit inside—the chest's opening is smaller than the submersible—but try as you might to get away, you're pulled closer and closer.

The water around you grows dark as a large funnel of debris forms, like the violent vortex of an undersea tornado.

And you're right in the middle of it.

You gulp, realizing there's no way out. The force of the vortex is going to pull your submersible apart.

Sure enough, hairline fractures appear on the submersible's window. The vortex pulls you towards the centre of the chest. It's grown larger—or have you been squashed into something smaller?

No time to think. No time to scream. You take a breath and gasp as the machine crunches and warps around you. Jets of high-pressure water punch into the interior of the submersible. You're swallowed up by darkness and—

Turn to page 1.

You can always come back to that chest later. What else is down here? You pilot the submersible farther along the edge of the abyss. *Is this where the scuba crew is exploring?* No, there's no way the divers are actually down there, is there? This thing is so deep it's scary.

You throw the submersible into reverse. Maybe it's worth checking out that chest after all . . .

But then, amazingly, you notice a light emanating from deep within the chasm. You pilot the sub back over to it, straining to see the divers. Instead, you see something large rise from the depths. Its protrusions undulate in the deep waters, and the glow gets stronger as it rises. Wow! It's some kind of bioluminescent sea creature.

As the thing approaches, you stare at it from the safety of your submersible. It's at least twice the size of your sub and seems to be half-octopus, half-jellyfish. It floats above the chasm.

You search for a remote camera on the sub, and when you find it, you quickly snap a photo, giving off a massive flash of light.

"Oops."

The creature whirls around in the water. You're not

sure where its eyes are, but as it tilts its bottom towards you, angrily extending its tentacles, you see that it's got an enormous, sharp-looking beak.

Then it opens its beak, and you can see all the way into its gullet.

Is that—a *scuba tank* in there?

"Oh no," you say, and reverse the sub immediately. You've got to get out of here, right?

No, you realize. The submersible is too slow. You've got to stay and fight. But how?

If you use your grappling claws, turn to page 40.

If you try to startle it with more flashes of light, turn to page 43.

02:08

As the lobsters close in on you, you tense your muscles and make a move towards the left, because LEFT IS BEST.

Left, it turns out, is also where the slickest biofilm on the rocks is, which means that you—

"YEEEEARGH!"

—smack down onto them. But you manage to catch yourself before you go flying over the edge of the cliff.

You scramble to get up. You're covered in sea water and biofilm, but you can do this. You can beat these lobsters at their own game—

URGH. You feel the massive crusher claw of the closest lobster clamp down on you. Hard. Then the lobster hoists you out over the jagged rocks below. You try to reach into the gap between the lobster's claws to pry them open, but it's like trying to force apart steel beams.

Then you start getting closer and closer to the lobster's moving mouthparts.

You *did* want a lobster dinner on your trip to the east coast, but this isn't quite the one you had in mind.

THE END.

To try again, go back to page 104.

The lobsters keep charging at you in that awkward way that only lobsters can, scuttling quickly over the rocks. Just as they're about to jab you with the sharp ends of those claws, you hurl yourself to the right, leaping off your feet and landing in a crumpled heap on some of the smaller rocks.

The lobsters don't even have time to track your movements. They must see the cliff approaching, because they try to reverse their course. But these crustaceans are so massive that momentum pushes them forward, over the edge of the cliff, and—

CRUNCH.

Yowzers! Are they still in one piece?

Fighting the pain that's flaring all over your body, you push yourself back onto your feet and stagger to the cliff.

You carefully peer over the edge just long enough to confirm that, yup, those lobsters won't be a problem for you anymore.

"If only I had a massive pot of boiling water," you think aloud. You could feed a whole town with those claws and tails. Think of the chowder you could make! And boy do you love lobster chowder.

But once your interest in eating the mighty lobsters subsides, you move away from the carnage below and turn back to the rocky path leading to the shore.

Still, you can't help but think about those lobsters as you walk. *How did they get so big? Is it possible they were engineered to be that way?* They sure did seem like they were there on purpose. And what if their purpose was to keep you away from the treasure, like some kind of mutant guard dogs?

You round a corner and stop in your tracks.

Once again, you're staring at oversized mutant animals. Only this time, it's a group of six or seven giant oysters—each easily the size of a small car. They're in a cove, basking in a pool of sea water that filters in and out with each wave.

"No way," you say, and take a few steps forward.

Then it hits you. As the oysters open and close their huge hinged shells, you spot a gleaming white orb inside each one.

Pearls! Perfect in every way, only far bigger than anything that could ever occur in nature. These massive pearls are as big as basketballs.

So *that's* what the lobsters were hiding.

Great, you think. You've found the treasure. All you need to do is jam something in between their open shells and pull out the pearls. Then, you figure, you won't be needing any kind of money ever again.

Thinking quickly, you spot a piece of driftwood on the rocks nearby. You grab it and wedge it into the nearest oyster's massive mantle. You hope it's strong enough to hold, then, taking a deep breath, you plunge your arms into the slimy, wet tissue. *Urgh! People eat these things raw?*

You feel the oyster trying to snap its two halves shut, quickly wrap your hands around the pearl, yank it back, and—

SNAP!

Heart in your throat, you go flying as the oyster cracks through the driftwood. Then you look down and sigh with relief. In your hands is a huge white orb that must be worth . . . thousands? Millions?

And there's more where that came from!

00:00

You survived! There are eleven other ways to escape the danger—try to find them all!

You decide the boulder is too far away for you to get to it safely. You make a break for the island instead. Behind you, the engine cuts. You wonder if Erin has spotted the map. Sure enough, the speedboat's engine revs again, but slower this time.

It's nearly impossible to see the boat in the strange, soupy haze of fog that hangs over the island. And there's something about it you don't like or trust. It's almost like the fog seeks you out, cloaking you in its thick whitish clouds.

Ouch! Your leg catches on a sharp underwater rock. You narrow your eyes and peer through the mist. You can only just see a vague outline of the island. You keep moving in its direction.

As you finally reach land, you hear a loud scrape and crunch. You manage a smile. Erin's boat didn't make the landing she wanted.

You follow the sound of Erin's splashing and cursing as you move slowly among the sharp rocks of the shoreline. The fog will keep you hidden for now.

Turn to page 45.

SOS is the way to go. Is it three short blasts, three long blasts and back to three short blasts again, or the other way around? You realize a) it doesn't matter—because they'll blend together, but more importantly, b) you've got to send it out, *now*!

You pull on the chain, and even though there's a wall separating you from the horn, the sound is still ear-splitting. You release the chain and the sound stops.

You hear the men getting closer. You'd better get back to the signal. So you pull on the chain. Three short blasts. Three long blasts. And then three more short blasts.

Then you realize—*dang*—there's no way anyone is going to come to your rescue before these guys catch you.

But no sooner do you finish using the foghorn than the ocean begins to froth and boil like there's something *big* emerging from it.

"What the—?"

SPLASH! One gigantic tentacle punches out of the violently churning waters. Then another. And another. You count eight in all. They're at least the girth of tree trunks, and even longer! The sticky suckers at the ends of them attach to the jagged rocks and pull the bulk of a huge octopus-like creature from the depths.

You hear another sound. A screaming sound. It takes you a second to realize that you're the one making it.

That may not be your best strategy to avoid being seen by this creature. The thing zeroes in on you standing there screaming beside an open window, and it immediately clambers across the rocks with lightning-like speed. It latches on to the outer edge of the light-house and pulls itself up towards you.

You turn to run, then remember those guys are blocking your path. So you turn back to face the sea creature, trying to figure out your strategy.

The monster looks at you. It slowly, carefully extends a tentacle to the window.

Wait. What?

You freeze, expecting the monster to wrap its tenta-cles around the shaft of the lighthouse and break it off.

But the monster just pauses and waits.

And then you realize what's happening. "I put out the SOS," you say. Can this creature actually *understand* Morse code?

It extends another tentacle to the window you're standing beside, and you climb out the window and slide down the tentacle until you're safely on its back.

Down below, you see your three would-be captors

staring in shock as you're whisked away from the rocky outcrop near the lighthouse and into the Atlantic.

The creature makes sure to hold the upper portion of its back above water, keeping you safe and dry. The question is, what do you do with a friendly monster octopus at your beck and call? Search for the treasure? Your parents? Scare everybody in town?

Who knows, maybe all three.

Sounds like a great way to cap off the weirdest day you've ever had.

00:00

You survived! There are eleven other ways to escape the danger— try to find them all!

Without giving it another thought, you open the lid of the chest on the left, and—

"NO WAY! IT'S THE TREASURE!" you yell.

And you can't take your eyes off it. The chest is bursting with all manner of glittering jewels and golden trinkets. But—hold up a second—what is it doing down here at the bottom of a cavern? And how did whoever put it here get back out?

Hmm. Maybe the answers are close by. Like, in that second chest.

You take a deep breath, reach forward to open it, and—

There's nothing there.

You're not sure why one treasure chest would be loaded to the brim and the other empty. Except maybe it's not empty, is it? Reaching inside and feeling around for a moment, you pull out a tiny metal whistle.

"That's unusual," you say, as if the rest of your day has been completely normal.

Then—because what else do you do with a whistle—you bring it to your lips and blow.

You hear nothing. Maybe it's one of those whistles that only dogs can hear. But there are no dogs in this cavern. Or above ground. Or—

CRUNCH!

You look up to see a new shaft of light piercing through the wall of the cavern.

The lobsters! They're moving the rocks out of the way.

You freak out, and in doing so, blow the whistle again.

The lobsters stop what they are doing. They look your way. One of them freezes with its massive claws in mid-air.

And then you put it together: *Does this whistle command the lobsters?*

You blow on it again. The lobsters resume moving rocks out of the way. In doing so, they reveal a series of stone steps that would allow you to walk back up to the pathway.

You grab as many jewels as you can carry, then move towards the steps and begin to make your way out, keeping a watchful eye on the monstrous crustaceans.

Somebody clearly put the treasure here. Probably even put these lobsters here to guard it. You're not sure who. But as long as you keep blowing that whistle, it doesn't really matter.

00:00

You survived! There are eleven other ways to escape the danger— try to find them all!

You wiggle your index finger back and forth between the two chests, then decide upon the one on the right.

Reaching down, you pull back the lid. Given that it's barely light enough to see the chests, you're not surprised that the interior is completely dark. You feel your hand around the void, hoping your fingers will connect with untold riches. Could it be jewels? Bars of gold? Valuable coins?

But you get NOTHING.

Holding your hand there for a minute, it occurs to you that you've stretched your arm into the chest nearly up to your shoulder. Which, of course, is impossible.

You gasp, realizing that you should probably pull your arm out right now, when—

You find yourself being swallowed up by total darkness once again.

Another cavern? Inside the chest?

And then you open your eyes.

You're sitting in a room. It's an office of some kind. There's a computer in front of you. A document is open on the screen. You stare at the document. You see these words. Like, the ones you are reading right now.

"What the?" you start.

And then you see "What the?" appear on the screen.

You look down.

You're the one typing.

You're typing the words *right now*.

STOP TYPING THE WORDS, you think.

But you just end up typing in angry capital letters.

Then you turn away. You look into a mirror on the wall. You gasp. You're not you anymore.

You're him.

You're the author, Jeff Szpirglas.

And that's when you open your mouth and scream the most blood-curdling scream of them all.

THE END.

To try again, go back to page 104.

You yank on the chain. A booming sound fills the room, and you nearly jump out of your shoes.

You let go of the chain for a moment, and the sound stops. Now all you hear is a loud ringing in both ears.

Then you pull it again, and the intense sound fills the room for a second time. That ought to do the trick!

Satisfied help will arrive soon, you let go of the chain and head to the stairs, hoping you can dodge the men and make it back outside. But they're already on their way up. Cornered and hoping they haven't seen you, you begin to race towards the top of the lighthouse.

You run feverishly, but as you reach one of the windows overlooking the ocean, you pause.

Something's grabbed your attention. It's moving in the waters outside, and it's *big*.

SPLASH! A massive tentacle punches out of the ocean and slaps against the wet rocks. Then another tentacle. And another! They're all thicker than tree trunks. And they pull the rest of the creature they belong to out of the Atlantic and onto land.

The thing looks like it's half-octopus, half-monster—and totally annoyed. It easily dwarfs the boat that's anchored outside, which means it could swallow you whole for a light snack. It fixes its five eyes on the light-house, opens its beak-like mouth, and roars.

You immediately recognize the noise escaping its mouth. It's the same deep sound that came from the foghorn. And as the creature pulls itself along the rocky shore towards the lighthouse, you suddenly understand where all those fish bones came from. This is perhaps not the first time this monstrous thing has come ashore.

You look back down the stairwell. The men seem to have forgotten about you and are tearing towards the open door below.

They might have the right idea, especially if this thing is slower on land than it is in the water. Then again, how can it possibly reach you at the top of the lighthouse?

If you race back downstairs, turn to page 81.
If you head to the top of the lighthouse, turn to page 82.

You jerk the boat sharply to the left, because, hey, you're left-handed.

Lefties always get the worst of everything: your writing smears across pages when you use a pencil, there are never enough left-handed hockey sticks in the sporting-goods store and there are certainly never enough left-handed scissors in the bin at school. Lefties always lose out!

But not today. This is the day when your left-handed instincts are going to save you and Erin, because left is best!

Also left, as it turns out, are more rocks.

These rocks are big and jagged, and Erin's boat crashes into them very impressively.

At least nobody's going to bother you about being left-handed anymore.

THE END.

To try again, go back to page 96.

Instinctively, you yank hard on the wheel, cutting right. The manoeuvre slows you down, but you're still headed towards the sea caves dead ahead.

In fact, so is that plane—

Shouldn't the pilot at least try to steer away?

Too late—with a loud bang, the plane's wing smashes against the rocks above the sea cave.

"Watch out!" Erin screams, as flaming debris rains down on you. This time it's Erin who takes the wheel and steers you to safety, just in the nick of time.

You're leaning over the side of the boat, trying to catch your breath and not lose your lunch, when something catches your attention. Under the water, nestled in the rocks, you see something gleaming. Something metal. Something golden.

You're about to say something to Erin when your attention is taken by the wreck several metres away. The seaplane is partially submerged, and it looks like the fuselage has caught fire.

It's too far away to do any damage to Erin's boat, but then, through the fog, you see a glimmer of movement on the rocks between the boat and the plane. A man is suspended over the water, hanging from a parachute that's tangled in the jagged rocks. The pilot must have ejected before the crash!

You watch the pilot struggle to cut himself free of the parachute lines. He manages to slice through a couple of them, but then the knife slips from his hand, falling onto a rock sitting in the water below.

You turn to Erin, who's standing by the wheel. "Should we at least help him down?"

Erin shakes her head. "Sorry, kid. He was trying to kill us a few minutes ago. Besides, he's far enough away from the plane that even if it explodes he'll probably be fine. I'll tell you what, though: if he's still there after we get the treasure, I'll send one of my people to get him."

She's got a point, but you're not sure you can just leave him up there for hours, or maybe longer. It would only take a few minutes to toss the knife back up to him, wouldn't it?

If you help the pilot, turn to page 76.

If you leave the pilot hanging, turn to page 79.

You're a sitting duck out here. At least inside you'll stand a chance of dodging these guys.

So you rush towards the lighthouse and look up. It towers over you. Partway up the tall cylindrical structure there's a metal cone jutting out the side. *What the heck?* You wish you knew something about how lighthouses worked.

You're at the entrance now, and you heave on the old iron door with all your might. It squeals open and you stumble into the dimly lit lower chamber.

The place has an old, rotten, fishy smell. You wonder if something might have crawled in here and died. You choke as you reach around for any kind of light switch. Your fingers feel an old breaker on the wall. You give it a pull, and—

From somewhere in the bowels of the lighthouse, you hear something chug to uneasy life. Above you, old lights flicker on. It's a miracle anything still works in this place, but the little light you have is enough to spy an old, discarded flare gun in the corner. You rush over and grab it, then make your way to the winding staircase that goes directly up the centre of the lighthouse.

You look up. A shaft of light from outside penetrates down to the murky depths.

Just then, your ears pick up talking. It sounds like the men are just outside the door, but it's hard to fully hear them with that engine rattling. They must know you're in here, and there's only one way to go: up.

So you start to race up the steps, but you're feeling winded after only a few rotations around the rickety old staircase.

You look ahead, and a little ways up you spy a small room built off the side of the lighthouse. It's not lit, but it might be big enough to hide in. Plus, it would give you a break from these stairs. Or you can try to put more distance between yourself and Captain John's crew.

If you hide inside the room, turn to page 54.

If you keep climbing the stairs, turn to page 56.

You'd be a sitting duck in that lighthouse. Better to hide out here. Besides, you can see some dark clouds and a bank of fog moving in. If you're lucky, it will help you make your escape.

You crouch behind a large patch of boulders as you watch the boat pull in and the men splash onto shore.

You feel a sudden cool breeze and start to shiver. You wrap your arms around yourself and try to rub some heat back into your wet skin.

"Don't mind the chill, matey," a voice calls out. "I have that effect on people."

You jump and let out a small yelp.

Standing right in front of you is a man dressed in old-fashioned, ragged-looking clothing. He's got a patch over one eye, a hook for a hand and the most horrifying beard you've ever seen. Large warts protrude from his face and poke through the shaggy hair, which stretches all the way down to his chest. And then you realize— he's not standing.

He's floating.

You take a deep breath.

And you can see right through him.

"G-G-G-GHOST!" you scream.

You keep screaming, although you try to cover your mouth to keep from being too loud.

The man rolls his eyes and folds his arms across his chest. "Are you through yet?"

A minute later, you probably are. The ghost is still there, and he extends a hand for you to shake. Instinctively you reach out, and your hand passes right through his.

"Er, sorry 'bout that," he says. "I don't interact with the living much anymore. The name's Feared Beard."

"Feared Beard?" you repeat, aghast.

"On account of me terrifying beard," he says, matter-of-factly. Then he twists his nose, and on cue all of the hairs of his beard stand on end like they're porcupine quills. The bumps and warts on his face squirm around like they're *actual worms*. It's the most disgusting thing you've ever seen. He moves towards you, pushing that horrifying beard closer and closer . . .

. . . and asks: "So, what brings you to this miserable place?"

You open your mouth to answer, then pause. Maybe that isn't such a good idea.

If you keep talking to Feared Beard, turn to page 62.
If you ignore him, turn to page 68.

The salt water stings the cut on your ankle, but it's either that or getting captured . . . or annoyed to death by Feared Beard. Plus, it shouldn't take you that long to find the boat those guys left anchored by the island.

It's hard to tell how much time is passing while you swim through the ocean, but soon the ground drops away and the current forces you into deeper waters. The fog is so thick now that you've lost sight of any land.

Great. Just great. You're not even sure whether you're swimming back towards the shore or farther out to sea.

As you keep trying to get your bearings, you begin to panic. Just then, you see something bobbing up and down in the distance.

Phew. That must be the boat. You swim towards it. As you do, you see it in closer detail. It's not the same boat. No matter—this is your only option now.

"Hey! I'm over here!" you shout.

You're probably still too far away for anyone to hear you. You wonder if this is a fishing boat, because it's got a ton of gear on board—including a big cage on the back. Big enough for a person to fit inside, for sure.

You keep swimming towards it. "I'm over here. I need help!"

Then you see something in the misty waters. A fin? You whirl around. It disappears from view, ducking below you.

You turn back to the boat, and you can't believe you didn't recognize it immediately—you love Shark Week! That's no fishing boat; it's a research vessel. That thing hanging off the back? A shark cage.

And you're in the water, bleeding.

"Oh no," you breathe.

You begin to paddle madly for the boat, but then you notice something just below the surface. A large shape moving your way. Two large shapes. Make that three. Through the waters, you see rows of massive teeth coming at you.

You try to splash out of the way, but the great whites come rushing up from the depths, and—

CHOMP!

THE END.
To try again, go back to page 136.

COUNTDOWN TO EVEN MORE DANGER . . .

Can you survive?

30 MINUTES. 30 ENDINGS. YOU CHOOSE IF YOU LIVE OR DIE.